GRUDGE MOUNTAIN

Also by Albert Payson Terhune
in Large Print:

Lad: A Dog
Lad of Sunnybank
The Way of a Dog

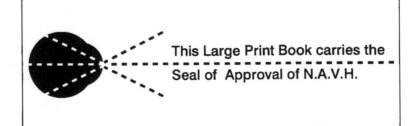

ALBERT PAYSON TERHUNE

GRUDGE MOUNTAIN

G.K. Hall & Co. • Thorndike, Maine

Published in 2000 by arrangement with HarperCollins Publishers, Inc.

G.K. Hall Large Print Perennial Bestseller Series.

The text of this Large Print edition is unabridged.
Other aspects of the book may vary from the original edition.

Set in 16 pt. Plantin by Minnie B. Raven.

Printed in the United States on permanent paper.

Library of Congress Cataloging-in-Publication Data

Terhune, Albert Payson, 1872–1942.
     Grudge mountain / by Albert Payson Terhune.
         p.   (large print)   cm.
     ISBN 0-7838-8744-2 (lg. print : hc : alk. paper)
     1. Collie — Fiction.   2. Dogs — Fiction.   3. Large type books.
     I. Title.
PS3539.E65 G78   2000
  813′.52—dc21   99-046902

This Book Is Dedicated to the Memory
of My Old-time Comrade,
SUNNYBANK GRAY DAWN
(1918–1929)

Chapter 1

The big collie came to a sliding halt and sniffed the ice-clear air. Then he barked, fiercely, in quick suspicion.

The morning sun blazed down on his dappled gray coat, turning it to spun silver, and its ruff and frill to glinting snow.

The man behind him halted, too, at this odd behavior of his dog. Guy Manell and Gray Dawn had been chums for three years, out in the loneliness of the Sierras. In that time, Guy had learned not to disregard his collie's rare instincts.

Thus, instead of laughing at the dog or bidding him move on, Manell scanned the tumble of mountains about him for cause of this sudden excitement.

Man and dog were standing midway of a steeply slanted trail that cut its snakelike course across the lower face of an egregious elephant-gray mountainside. All around towered other mountains of like hue and ruggedness. Not these the benignly swelling green mountains of the East, but grim and gaunt and ragged-topped forbidding peaks strewn and huddled and strung out in awesome grandeur.

To eastward, far away, Guy could glimpse the softer slopes that stretched toward the Persian

7

carpet of the hazy Mohave Desert. Here the dull gray was smeared with vast splashes of fiery orange and of vivid purple and dirty yellow, where Nature's immense paintbrush had smeared five-acre strokes of poppy and of lupin on the dun canvas of rocky background, or had covered square miles of wasteland with the ginger-yellow of wild buckwheat.

Below and behind man and dog was a tiny cup of land that nestled greenly at the base of several all-but-converging crags. Like an emerald lay the fertile area of bottom-land, with the silver brook that traversed it and with the snug little white cottage and clump of outbuildings.

That tidy white cottage, far below, was Guy Manell's home — his ranch house. The emerald-green cup and the gentle slopes that ringed it in were Guy Manell's raisin-grape ranch.

For three years, now, he had dwelt here. The rich little ranch was beginning to reward his skilled toil by bringing him prosperity. Fantastically, by reason of its contrast with the harsher and higher ground about it, he had named his home-acres "Friendly Valley."

Never was the contrast keener than when he stood where today he stood, on the hillslope midway between his ranch and the tallest and grimmest and gloomiest peak in all that waste of tall and grim and gloomy peaks — the sinister crest of Grudge Mountain.

Gray Dawn was facing this mountain, now. He had begun to alternate his sniffs with low growls,

8

far down in his throat. Suddenly he broke again into a fanfare of raucous barks. He bounded forward over the rough trail, toward the furlong-distant point where the path made a sharp turn and zigzagged upward over the rugged hip of Grudge Mountain.

The man followed, genuinely curious. Not thus did his silver-gray collie announce the vicinity of ground-squirrel or skunk or other ordinary animal. Manell was inquisitive as to what could cause the stark excitement.

As the dog neared the bend, Guy whistled him to a halt, until he himself should come alongside. Together they rounded the boulder at the trail's turn, the collie tugging to break free from Manell's detaining fingers in his white ruff.

Overhead soared the gray rock wall, far above the neighboring peaks — bald, scarred, scowling. Yet Nature seemed to have repented her of creating a mountain of such unrelieved grimness. For its oddly squared summit bore traces of lush verdure along the nearer edges, as if there might be a rich plateau — impossible as was the idea — on the table-land crest. No man could prove or disprove this idea. For no man, in local history, had been able to scale Grudge Mountain to its elusive peak.

True, a precipitous groove, in the face of the cliff, seared the blank face of the wall for several hundred feet, rising from the tumble of foothills near the mountain's base. But this groove ended abruptly when it reached the higher of the two outjutting ledges which flared forth, one above and to the left of the other. Above and beyond the upper ledge appeared no foothold for man or beast.

The dog no longer was sniffing and listening. No further need now for his miraculously keen scent and hearing. His nearsighted eyes at last could see what had so excited him.

Following the direction of Gray Dawn's interested gaze, Guy beheld a smallish figure crouched tremblingly among the welter of trailside rocks, not a hundred feet ahead of him.

The figure was a boy's. The youth had his back to the man and the collie. He was peering nervously toward another bend of the trail, some fifty yards ahead of him. There were terror and sheer misery in the slumping pose and in the droop of the sombrero-crowned little head.

Guy strode forward, the dog still held in fretting restraint. The wind set from the other direction; and the man's moccasined feet made little noise on the stony trail. Thus he was within a few yards of the lad before his approach was noted. Then, a pebble upturned by the collie's scrambling toenails made the unhappy boy turn around with a start of fear.

The sudden apparition of Guy and Gray Dawn, so unexpectedly close to him, was too much for the youth's jangled nerves. His tanned young face went scarlet, then dead white. Before Guy could speak, the boy whipped out an absurdly small revolver from the breast of his flannel shirt and leveled it at him.

For an instant, Manell blinked bemusedly at the white young face with its delicate features and despairingly fierce eyes, and at the pistol held so wabblingly in menace.

Surprise made Guy loosen his hold, instinctively, on Gray Dawn's furry ruff. The collie took advantage of his freedom to trot inquiringly up to the pistol-wielder, tail awag, eyes friendly.

Even in the astonishment of the moment, Guy found scope to wonder at this unwonted action on the part of his usually standoffish dog. Dawn was Manell's own chum and worshipper. He was coldly civil to Guy's few friends and to his workmen. But toward strangers, as a rule, he was aloof and more than indifferent.

The sole exceptions to this line of conduct were toward the few Shoshone Indians still remaining in the region. To these natives Gray Dawn was actively and hysterically hostile. Even as certain dogs, otherwise gentle, fly into an unreasoning rage at sight and scent of a negro, so Gray Dawn was the unreasoningly murderous foe of any Indian he chanced to meet. The trait is not rare among western dogs.

Never had the collie advanced in actively friendly fashion toward any person whom he encountered for the first time. Yet now, with plumed tail waving and every inch of his shining gray body eloquent of hospitable cordiality, he was greeting this gun-toting boy with real effusion.

The lad glanced quickly down at the dog. He saw that Gray Dawn was not likely to attack. So he resumed his defiant glare at Manell.

The humor of the situation took hold of Guy. In that peaceful neighborhood practically no one nowadays carried a weapon or had need for one. Yet the boy was covering him with his ludicrously inadequate pistol in true Wild-West fashion. Yes, and his clothes were of the movie Wild-West type, too, from his picturesque sombrero to his polished high boots.

"Sonny," said Manell, breaking the tense moment of silence, "if you're holding me up, you'll find I assay just now one nickel watch and a pipe and tobacco pouch and six bits in ready cash. If you pulled that pop-gun because you think I was planning to hold *you* up, let me set your mind at rest. I couldn't get into those sample size clothes of yours; even if I could stand the laugh I'd get for wearing them. So suppose you park the pistol and calm down. If you shot me with that thing, and if I ever happened to find it out, I'd probably lose my temper and spank you. So —"

He got no farther. The boy seemed all at once to understand the silliness of his own melodramatic action. That or else Manell's words and voice showed him the uselessness of his fright.

He lowered the gun, sticking it shamefacedly back into his brand-new flannel shirt. Then, in a trice, his over-taut nerves went to pieces.

Gray Dawn had thrust his nose into the lad's palm, in token of friendliness. The touch made the boy jump. The white face went scarlet again. With a catching little sob he flung himself on the ground, his arms around the collie's shaggy neck.

Burying his face in the dog's white ruff, the youngster burst into uncontrollable weeping.

"*Oh!*" he sobbed, as Gray Dawn sought frantically to lick the tear-stained visage. "Oh, it's all so horrible! — So *horrible!*"

Disgust swept away Guy's momentary amusement.

"You big bullcalf!" he scoffed. "Stop bellowing like a sick baby. Buck up! Be a man, can't you?"

"No," wailed the youth, "I can't. I wish to heaven I could! I —"

"Could *what?*" demanded Manell, with increasing contempt at the babyish display of tears. "What do you 'wish to heaven' you could do? If —"

"I wish to heaven I *could* be a man!" wept the other, lifting a red and wet face from the dog's ruff. "But I can't. You see, I'm — I'm a girl!"

"Good Lord!" blithered Guy, staring, jaw adroop, down on the pitiful little figure at his feet. "So — why, so you are!"

Chapter 2

For an instant neither of them spoke. The girl's sobs grew fainter. She was making a gallant fight for self-possession.

Gray Dawn, in his eager effort to lick the unhappy face, managed to nuzzle her sombrero to one side. It fell off, revealing a crown of high-piled sunny hair that had been tucked under it.

Instantly, with this revelation, the weeper ceased to bear the slightest resemblance to a half-grown boy, and became a decidedly pretty girl in sprucely up-to-date camping attire. The transformation was magical.

"I'm sorry!" mumbled Guy, confusedly. "I — I didn't mean — I didn't mean to —"

"You needn't be sorry," she disclaimed, getting to her feet and wiping her eyes. "It *was* babyish of me. If it's babyish for a boy to cry, it's just every bit as babyish for a grown woman to cry. But —"

She stopped, with a shudder and an apprehensive glance up the trail toward the bend.

"Something frightened you?" ventured Guy. "I mean something before you saw us? You were looking over there so hard you never heard us coming. Was there anything — ?"

"Tell me," she interrupted him, "is it the

custom for people around here to wear burlap bags over their heads and faces — like a great brown shapeless mask?"

"Why, not that I ever heard of," answered Manell, puzzled. "Is it a joke?"

"I don't think so. He seemed in earnest. He —"

"He? Who?"

"My father and I have bought a ranch down yonder," with a backward jerk of her dainty head. "We're just getting settled. My father is Saul Graeme. My name is Klyda Graeme. We went out, this morning, to look for water. I mean, we went to hunt for some body of water we could pipe down to our ranch for irrigating. Dad thought there must be a lake or a pond or a big spring, up on top of this mountain. On account of the green that grows out over the edge. We couldn't find any trail going up there. So I tramped around one side of the base while he tramped around the other, looking for one. Just as I got here, on my way back, I heard someone behind me."

Again that queer reminiscent shudder made her pause. Forcing it down, she continued:

"I looked back. There, about midway between me and that bend, somebody was coming toward me. It was a man — at least I suppose it was a man; though it looked more like the kind of animal I've seen in nightmares. He was bent double — I suppose so as to be hidden from me by the rocks. So I couldn't get any clear idea of his clothes. But, over his head and shoulders, he was

15

wearing a huge shapeless burlap bag — or something that looked like it. It hadn't any eye-holes in it. It may not have been a bag at all. It — it may just have been his head."

"But —"

"I caught sight of him, in that gap where the rocks fall away on each side of the trail. I suppose I must have cried out or made some sort of noise that he heard and that let him know I had seen him. For he stopped creeping stealthily and began to run toward me, all stooped over on all fours — and with that hideous bag-thing still flapping in front of his face. It was — Ugh!"

Guy Manell frowned perplexedly up the trail. The story he had heard did not make sense. In twentieth-century California — outside of motion pictures — folk do not creep, on all fours, through the rocks, seeking by clumsy disguises to scare harmless strangers. Only an eccentric madman would be likely to do such a thing.

Yet he could not doubt the mortal sincerity of Klyda Graeme's narrative. The girl was in very evident earnest. As he pondered, she went on:

"I suppose I was tired from my long tramp. Perhaps the grimness of these giant mountains had begun to get on my nerves. You see, my father and I are new to all this. Anyhow, the sight of that brown-masked weird figure frightened me as I've never been frightened before. I snatched out the pistol Dad told me to carry when I went on mountain walks; and I aimed it at him."

"Well?"

"Well, he stopped short. Then he took a step forward again. Just then I heard the bark of a dog — this lovely big gray collie of yours, I suppose. He heard it, too. For he turned around and — and just vanished. He didn't run away. He seemed to melt into the air. Of course he must have crouched down behind the rocks and made his way back around the bend. But he did it so quickly, so silently — ! I was looking after him and trying not to feel as if I'd seen a ghost or a mountain goblin — when I heard something behind me. It was so sudden, it seemed to me as if you must be the same man, straightened up and with the bag taken off his face."

"I?"

"Yes, I know it was idiotic of me. But my nerves were all in a mess. I'm so ashamed, Mr. — Mr. —"

"Manell," he answered. "Guy Manell."

"Oh!" cried Klyda. "Then you're a neighbor of ours. At least, I suppose we'd count as neighbors, out here. We've bought the north corner of the Glohn ranch. It's only a mile or so from you, isn't it? Mr. Glohn told us about you; and —"

"You're the New England people — the people from the Berkshires — who are going to try raisin-growing on the Ojan slope?" broke in Guy. "One of my men said a family had bought that tract and that they were looking for labor to help reclaim the land for a vineyard. I've meant to ride over and welcome you. But up to a day or so ago I've been so busy I've had no time to. No

17

wonder you are looking for water! You'll need it badly enough, if you're going to irrigate even half of that hillside. Glohn used to say his part of the slope was so steep that everything rolled down off of it, except the mortgage. If I can be of any help —"

He checked himself, belatedly realizing that his comments on her new home were not precisely encouraging, nor tactful. She noted his embarrassment and ignored its cause.

"We skirted your land this morning, Dad and I," she said. "We arranged to meet at the edge of the road, by the brook, on our way home. It is so cool and shady and restful under those trees, after all this flood of sunlight! It's an ideal place to wait for anyone. Poor old Dad! If he didn't have any better success in climbing the mountain than I did, we'll have to begin our water-hunt all over."

"I never heard of anyone who succeeded in climbing Grudge Mountain," answered Guy. "Once in a blue moon, some tourist takes a try at it. And every now and then a Kern County rancher, hereabouts, tries to solve the water problem by a day or two of hunt for a way up. Nobody succeeds. Sometimes a rock-slide crushes the climber's skull. Back in Mexican days, Old Man Negley says, those patches of green, up there, roused the Greasers' lively imaginations. They quizzed the few Indians that they hadn't driven out of here, too. Between imagination and the lies the Shoshones told them, they

pieced together a yarn of a beautiful moun-
taintop lake and a tribe of godlike men who lived
up there on its banks, and all sorts of drivel of the
same kind."

"You say it's called Grudge Mountain? Is —"

"That's part of the yarn. It seems one Mexican
soldier of fortune — a lieutenant of Peg-Leg
Santa Ana, I believe — was so fired with the tales
that he decided to explore the lake and to annex
the unknown table-land to Mexico. He tried to
climb by a series of ropes fastened to stakes that
his men drove into the rock-faults, and by
noosing the outjuts above him. When he was
two-thirds of the way up, the rope broke, not six
inches above his hands. Down he came — all that
was left of him. His men declared the rope was
not broken, but cut —"

"Cut? But how — ?"

"That's the point. It couldn't be, of course.
For it was parted, only a few inches above him,
against the bare face of the rock. But the soldiers
clung to the story, as soldiers will — especially
Greaser soldiers. An Indian told them the mountain didn't want to be climbed — that it cut the
rope itself in some mystic way, to keep from
being explored — that it grudged anyone discov-
ering its summit. And 'Grudge Mountain' it has
been, from that day."

"What a perfectly mad yarn!"

"Isn't it? But it's sane platitude, compared
with the stories that used to appear at intervals in
the newspapers, thirty years or so ago, about the

19

'Enchanted Mesa,' in Arizona. That was a broad table-land on top of an unscalable mountain, you know.

"People claimed it was an ancient city that had lost touch with the rest of the world, thousands of years ago, when some earthquake turned its slopes to precipices. They said a race of prehistoric men still inhabited it. Even scientists believed that."

"I've read about the Enchanted Mesa, somewhere," said Klyda. "Long ago. In an old magazine, I think. I remember it by the queer photographs of the mesa. It stood up from the plain like an irregular oversized block of ice. Has it never been climbed?"

"Dozens of expeditions, big and small, tried the job. They couldn't make it. But some of the climbers who got nearest the top — or least far from it — swore they could see queer human faces peering down at them from over the edge. Faces like none others they had known or imagined."

"What kind of faces?"

"That's the question. No two of the climbers could agree on what the mesa people looked like. The descriptions covered every possible type, from ape faces with horns and tusks to pure Nordic. And no wonder they couldn't agree. For there weren't any faces at all."

"How do you know?" asked the girl, loath to have so fascinating a mystery swept into nothingness.

"Because at last one man did get to the summit. He got there in much the same way the Mexican officer tried to climb Grudge Mountain. He found what may or may not have been signs of prehistoric civilization. But he found nothing worth the danger of the climb. No human or animal life, no wonder-city, no treasure. That was before the time of airplanes. Otherwise —"

"Airplanes!" exclaimed Klyda. "That's the answer! Has anyone ever tried to land on the summit of Grudge Mountain with an airship?"

"No," said Manell. "There isn't enough curiosity about it, nowadays. Eagen, of the Santa Barbara section — the forestry bureau, you know — told me he's passed above it, several times — at quite a distance, but near enough to see there's no big lake and no sign of life. That doesn't mean there aren't springs, though, or even deep little rock ponds, that could be tapped for irrigation. He was too far above to see those, if they are there."

As they talked, they had been moving by wordless consent down the trail in the direction whence Guy had come. The girl hesitated.

"I am taking you out of your way," she said. "You were coming up the trail when you met me; and we're going down it. I'm all right now; and I shan't be foolish enough to be frightened again or to draw a pistol on innocent strangers. Please don't bother to come any farther with me."

"I was wasting part of the morning on the

same errand that you were," he said, "and I can go back there any other time. I just happened to remember, a day or two ago, that the bottom of that groove, running up to the second ledge, is always more or less damp. That got me to wondering if there may not be a spring somewhere near the top of the groove, or perhaps under the lee of the ledge. I went to explore, yesterday. It was a stiff climb, up the groove; and most of it is choked with chaparral. But I was right. The ground there *is* damp; and the higher I went the damper it got. I had no hatchet or knife with me, to clear the underbrush and make any close examination. So this morning I came back," touching the short ax stuck in his belt, "to probe farther. But I started late; and the sun is getting hotter all the time. I'm glad enough of an excuse to put it off till early morning or early evening, some day."

"But what do you want of more water?" she queried, in perplexity. "Dad and I were looking at your ranch this morning from the road, by the bridge. It is a joy to the eye, in this half-arid part of the world. The grass is so fresh and green; and that little brook winding through the middle of your land —"

"It is," he assented. "You're right. By a miracle I hit on the two most desirable things in this vicinity — water to irrigate with and land that's worth irrigating. I have every drop of water that I need for my own uses and for my small vineyard. Just enough. But no more than enough."

"Then why do you want more? To lease the water rights to — ?"

"No. I'm thinking of buying that ninety-acre wedge, along the first rise of the hill, west of my little valley. If I do, I must find water to irrigate the vineyard I want to plant there. If I can't find enough water and a convenient way to get it to my vineyard, I shan't buy the land. That groove would make a marvelous natural conduit, for the worst of the distance. After that, there's a downward slope all the way to my very door."

"If —"

"If I can get the right quantity of water, Nature will pipe it for the toughest stretch of distance; and surface pipes will bring it the rest of the way at a low enough cost to make the job worth while. Outside my own tiny valley, there's no sense sinking a well, in this part of the Sierras. So if I can't get water from the groove or under the ledge, at Grudge Mountain, I shan't bother to take up that ninety-acre strip. . . . But I didn't mean to go preaching a sermon about my own plans," he finished, apologetically.

"I want to hear all about it," she insisted. "Because it concerns Dad and me, too. It's our problem as well as yours. My only objection to the 'sermon' is that so much talk about water makes me awfully thirsty. I meant to carry along a canteen, this morning; but I forgot. And all that hill-climbing, in the heat —"

"We'll be at my ranch in a few minutes, now," he said. "And you can get all the cool spring

23

water you want, to drink. We can wait in the shade on my porch till your father comes along. We can't miss seeing him if he passes the bridge, as you said. And it will be pleasanter for you to wait in a fairly comfortable porch chair than on the hard bridge rail."

"I'm putting you to ever so much trouble," she deprecated; nonetheless she was grateful for the invitation to rest and to slake her ever-increasing thirst.

Chapter 3

"You're giving me a legitimate excuse to loaf for a little while, during the heat of the day," he corrected. "Besides that, you're giving me my first chance in months to chat with a civilized girl. I'm your debtor for much. Suppose we let it go at that. By the way, when you have been out here a little longer and made a few hikes through these mountains, you'll learn that thirst is largely habit."

"A lifelong habit, I'm afraid."

"That's just it! A lifelong habit. From babyhood we're trained to go without things — to eat only three times a day, to go to sleep only at certain times, and all that. By the time we're grown up, most of us never even think of eating between meals or tumbling off to sleep at any time we happen to yawn. But thirst is the one and only physical or mental or moral impulse that nobody is trained to control, from babyhood. From the time we were kids we've always taken a drink of water when we thought we wanted one. We yelled from our cribs for it, at night, when we were babies. We've never tried to go without, or to drink only twice or three times a day. So when we are where we can't get water for two or three hours, we imagine we're suffering agonies of thirst. Instead, we're just suffering because we

25

can't yield, right away, to the thirst habit. Break the habit, and you'll be amazed to find how seldom you need to drink."

"I'll remember," she said meekly. "Only, if you don't mind, I won't begin to break the habit till I've had that cool spring water you promised me."

"Once or twice, in my hikes, I used to get lost, when I first came here," he rambled on, curiously glad to talk with this girl who seemed to have come to him out of his own past life in the eastern states, "and I used to think I should die of thirst. But the old-timers taught me how to find water."

"A divining rod?" she asked.

"A divining *bee*, for one thing," he replied. "If ever you're lost and can't find water, the first bee you run across will tell you where it is. Catch him and tie a thread around him. That will weigh him down and make him think he has his quota of honey. So he'll make a 'bee line' for his hive. Get the direction and follow it. The wild bees always have their hives as near as possible to running water. A simpler way is to walk downhill. At the very bottom of all steep mountains you're pretty sure to strike traces of water. Or, if it's near sunset, follow the wild doves. Almost always doves roost for the night within reach of water."

"Or," she suggested, with profound wisdom, nodding at Gray Dawn who ceased to trot just in front of them and bounded ahead, "follow the nearest beautiful big gray collie; and when he stops trotting and begins to canter, you'll know you're nearing a ranch house with a tremendously big glass of tremendously cool water waiting for a thirst-habit victim."

They laughed and quickened their pace. There, directly in front of them, lay the dip of emerald-green farmland, set deep in the grasp of the grim gray swirl of mountains.

A hundred yards away, across a billow of soft grass, nestled the trim white cottage, a story-and-a-half high; there were bougainvillæa and hibiscus and wisteria running riot over its walls and over the shallow adobe porch, and slovenly eucalyptus trees arching above. Beyond the cottage was a meadow, intersected by a winding brook and dotted with wide shade trees. On the far side of the dusty yellow byroad stretched the vineyards, rising gradually from the lush bottom-land until they ceased at the first stony ridge of the foothills.

Comfort, beauty, peace, modest prosperity, taste — the scene before them spoke of all these. Here was a farm, rather than a ranch — a farm that might have been picked up from the most fertile part of northern New Jersey and set down amid the harsh Sierra bleakness.

Calling an order through the window to his Chinese cook, as they passed the kitchen on the way to the porch, Guy led his guest to the hand-kerchief-sized veranda and drew forward for her a disreputable old Boston rocker of great age and ease. Installing her in this, he seated himself on the top step, at her feet.

"See," he said, pointing, "there is the bridge, and there is the road. Your father isn't here yet. When he comes in sight, we'll hail him. Now, isn't this better than sitting on the bridge to wait? . . . And here is Sing with the biggest water-pitcher in the whole shack. Also, you'll observe Gray Dawn twining himself around in front of him. Dawn's one holy ambition in life is to upset Sing when he's carrying something breakable. Some day he'll succeed. Dawn will never so much as look at Sing or pay any attention to him at all unless the Chink happens to be carrying something that will smash if he falls down."

The girl drank deep from the proffered glass. Then she sat fanning herself with her broadleaf sombrero. Lazily, Guy Manell watched her. Very pretty and very highbred she was, and dainty withal. He noted a steadiness of eye and a strength of chin that belied the softness of her mouth.

Klyda, far less noticeably, was taking a like observation of her host. She was tabulating the wide shoulders and the deep chest, the powerful middle-height figure, the square jaw, the pleasant brown eyes with their uncompromisingly direct look. She studied him, covertly. More and more she liked what the inspection and a native intuition told her.

Meantime, they talked as though they had known each other for years, he telling her of investing his small patrimony in this green cup of the Sierras and of making a paying venture of his vineyard within the first three years — a vineyard whose former owner had gone East in a fit of homesickness, just as his investment was beginning to pay.

"He was on the edge of a nerve-break," said Guy. "He used to repeat over and over to me:

" 'These here egregious mountains are doing funny things to my wits. Back home when you see a great big cloud-bank on the horizon and it climbs halfway up the sky, you know it's just clouds. But out here, you know it's mountain tops. That's agin nature. And the nearby mountains seem waiting to fall down on you. There's no friendliness to them. I've had enough of them to last me out my life. I'm going back to good old Kansas, where the worst thing that can happen to you is a cyclone or grasshoppers or drouths or dust-storms. Where it's flat enough, most places, to play billiards on. Gee, but I dream of Kansas, every night, and — and I wake up to see Grudge Mountain pyrooting above me and shutting out half the sky! I'm plumb homesick, in every inch of me. And I'm going to hotfoot it back to the place I'm homesick for.'

"I laughed at him. But I couldn't laugh very hard or very convincingly. For the same home-sickness would pull me back to Pompton Lakes in northern New Jersey, if I didn't tell it to shut up. . . . I warn you, you'll get to feeling that way about New England, if you stay on here long enough, Miss Graeme."

"Dad and I both feel like that, already," Klyda made wistful answer. "But we don't dare let ourselves get homesick. We aren't here because we like to be, but because we must."

Then she found herself telling of a father whose throat could not stand another eastern winter — who had come out here with her to try vine-growing in an experimental way until the dry mountain air should have healed his delicate larynx. She spoke gaily of her voluntary exile from home, and hopefully of the experiment they were trying.

Above them on all sides arose the giant mountains. Just to southward, and a thousand feet up, twisted the famed Ridge Road that skims the Sierra tops and links Los Angeles with Bakersfield.

Along it, silhouetted against the fire-blue sky, crawled an irregular succession of beetle-sized things whose black surfaces gave forth glints of sunlight. Motor-cars, these, on their way across the mountains. They seemed to hang perilously above the myriad chasms on every side of the gray-yellow thread of roadway.

Imperceptibly, the talk shifted back to the meeting of the man and the maid.

"How gloriously lucky it was that Gray Dawn happened to bark at that very instant!" said Klyda, stooping to pet the great silver-and-snow collie as he lay dozing at her feet. "If he hadn't —"

"I don't know, yet, why he did it," answered Guy. "He isn't given to that sort of thing, except to sound an alarm. The bark might have been a hail to you, if he caught your scent or the sound of your voice. But I can't understand why he growled so venomously, just afterward. He certainly wasn't growling at *you*. And it isn't like him to growl, for nothing. Yours wasn't the only sound or scent that the breeze brought to those uncanny ears or nostrils of his. There was something hostile — something he hated. That's the way he behaves when he meets a Shoshone or a —"

"It didn't look like an Indian, the creature that came toward me, with the burlap thing over its head," she contradicted. "It looked like — like — like nothing I ever saw before. Besides, is that the way an Indian — ?"

"It certainly is not," he agreed. "But whatever it was, Dawn got its scent or sound; and he didn't like it. You mustn't let one such happening prejudice you against our glorious country out here, Miss Graeme. This is a splendid region. The people in it are the kindliest, peacefullest, most neighborly —"

He checked his eulogy, as she started half out of her chair. At the same moment the mountain stillnesses were split by a distant explosion, half deadened by the stiff cross-breeze.

Something brushed lightly and with incalculable swiftness across the side of Manell's khaki shirt and thence with equal speed and lightness athwart the knuckle of his right hand that lay idly on the adobe step beside him.

There was a slurringly harsh spat-t-t on the adobe, close beside the idle hand. Guy looked down in hot annoyance.

"It was a shot!" Klyda exclaimed. "While you were talking, I happened to be looking over *there*," pointing to a mass of chaparral that fringed the scatter of big rocks at the entrance to Friendly Valley, more than two hundred yards behind them. "I saw a fluff of smoke from those bushes. Then came the report and —"

She did not finish her recital. Guy Manell was not listening. She followed the direction of his wide-staring eyes.

The man's gaze was riveted on the adobe step, directly alongside of him. Nor had he moved his hand which had been resting on the warm adobe. From the barked knuckle of its forefinger a drop or two of blood was beginning to ooze.

His khaki shirt, directly above the heart, was cut for perhaps two inches, as cleanly as if with a knife. Here the bullet had brushed, in passing — missing the flesh and spatting viciously against the adobe step. On its way it had grazed Manell's forefinger-knuckle.

The girl sprang up.

"Go indoors!" she exhorted. "He may fire again. Next time he may —"

But Guy did not heed nor hear. Mouth agape, eyes bulging, he sat and stared at the step, close beside his grazed hand.

There, flattened to the fantastic aspect of an inkblot, was the bullet, spent by its contact with the adobe. A few little spatters from it were lying an inch or so away.

The sunlight glittered and flashed from the flattened and ragged blob of metal, as it lay there. At the sight, Klyda forgot momentarily her fears for the man's safety. She forgot every-thing but the impossible object that glistened be-neath her gaze.

For the bullet was of gold — soft 24-carat "flour gold."

There it shone, like an evil fiery eye, on the dull grayish step, between them — the ball which so narrowly had missed Guy Manell's heart and which had grazed his hand — the bullet of virgin gold!

Chapter 4

"Gold!" sputtered Manell blankly. "It's — it's *gold!*"

He was handling the irregular golden wafer with almost superstitious astonishment, feeling it, between thumb and forefinger, holding it close to his eyes, tasting it, weighing it in his palm.

Klyda Graeme was scarcely less thrilled as she peered down at the flame-bright thing, in the sunglare. But, in a moment, common sense came to her aid.

Laying an imperative little hand on Guy's sleeve she exclaimed:

"Whatever it's made of, it's a bullet. It just missed killing you. The man who shot it may shoot again. Quick! Come farther back or else go indoors. Out here on the edge of the porch, you're a target for him. *Quick!*"

Impelled by her eager zeal in his behalf he got to his feet. He could not understand the queer stirring of his heart, at that urgent grasp of hers. For the time the odd new sensation not only blotted out any sense of his peril but also shifted his thoughts from the mystery of the golden bullet.

Instinctively, he did as she directed and

yielded to that impelling grip on his forearm. He moved back from the porch-steps to the veranda wall. There a corner of the house shut him off from view of the valley's rocky entrance whence the shot had been fired.

Klyda sighed in relief, as he stepped out of range of the peril.

"Good!" she breathed. "He can't see you from here. And there's no other cover, large enough to hide a man, within gun-range of where we are now. Who could — ?"

Her question remained unfinished. The man shook off the daze that had encompassed him. With it, unwittingly, he shook off her guiding hand from his shoulder. At a stride he had crossed the narrow porch; and at a second stride he had cleared the low steps.

"Stop!" she begged, in dismay. "Come back, out of sight! Oh, *what* are you doing? Stop!"

For, reaching ground, Manell had broken into a run, heading straight for the rocky tumble of undergrowth from which the shot had come.

"Wait there!" he shouted, over his shoulder, his face dark with sudden wrath. "I'll be back. Nobody's going to blaze at me and get away with it! I don't care whether his bullets are gold or diamond or radium. I'm going to overhaul him."

Despite her frightened appeals, he ran on, at top speed; the great gray collie dashing excitedly at his side and all but tripping him up in an effort to do his share in what Gray Dawn evidently deemed a highly interesting romp.

The girl saw Guy regain his balance, after barely missing a header as Gray Dawn swung directly across his path. Without checking his pace Manell called sharply to the dog:

"Back, Dawn! Go *home!*"

Instantly, the collie ceased gambolling and stared grievedly at his master.

Gray Dawn had been having a lovely time. And in the very midst of it, Guy had spoiled the galloping romp. Small wonder the dog looked beseechingly at him for a rescinding of the cruel order! These queer godlike humans forever were spoiling his fun.

But Guy did not rescind the command. Intent on his goal and on overhauling and punishing the would-be murderer who had shot at him from ambush, his one thought concerning his collie was to stop the dog from tripping him up and thus delaying his race for vengeance.

If he had been less absorbed in his wrathful quest he would have realized the invaluable aid Dawn could have furnished in tracking his secret assailant, through the thick brush and over the rock-masses.

As it was, the dog stood for a minute, gazing sorrowfully after his onrushing master. Then he turned back, tail and head adroop, toward the cottage. Much as he might mourn at Guy's mandate, it did not occur to the trained collie to disobey. Otherwise this story might not have been written.

Back to the porch Dawn wended his sad way.

As he neared the house he lost some of his air of dejection. For there, on the steps, shading her eyes as she watched Manell's headlong flight, stood the collie's new friend — this girl who understood so well how to rub him under the ears and to croon softly at him.

Gray Dawn quickened his dejected pace. Presently he ranged himself alongside her, on the adobe steps.

But she did not note Dawn's presence. Pale, wide-eyed, she was following breathlessly the course of Guy Manell's race toward the valley-entrance. At every step she half expected to see another puff of white smoke from the chaparral thickets and to see the rash pursuer roll over and over on the ground like a shot rabbit.

Deep down in her heart glowed a strange admiration for Guy's foolhardy courage in charging thus an armed and hidden enemy. There had been no bravado in his action — nothing but hot and righteous wrath that anyone should attack him in such cowardly manner — that, and an eagerness to catch and chastise the lurking homicide.

"Oh!" she murmured, unconsciously, to the silver collie, from between soft-parted lips. "He's a man! He's a *man!*"

Presently, she saw him reach the outer fringe of stone-strewn chaparral. Into it he plunged. For a moment or two she could see the dimming outlines of his body, as he crashed through the thickets. Then she could see only the tumbling of the manzanita-tops as he pushed his way among their ill-smelling stems. After that, there was no sign of him.

Klyda Graeme found herself trembling all over, but with eagerness rather than terror. Her hand, pressed to her heart, encountered the hard outlines of the pistol she had thrust into the breast of her outing shirt. The contact answered the question she had begun to ask herself, over and over again — the impotent question:

"Why can't I help him, instead of standing here, like this?"

No longer did she feel she was useless. With a weapon she could share his manhunt. She might even ward death from him should he come, unarmed, upon his hidden opponent.

She ran down the steps and across the meadow at as fast a pace as her tired limbs could muster. Straight for the valley-entrance she ran, the tiny pistol gripped tight in her hand.

Gray Dawn, deserted a second time, fidgeted and whimpered, from his place on the steps. Much he yearned to follow. But ever in his loyal mind sounded his master's injunction. "Go home!"

Wearily, the big collie lay down on the topmost step, his classic-chiseled head between his paws, his deepset sorrowful dark eyes on the flying figure of the girl. Life was so much bigger than were those who must live it!

Sing, the Chinese cook, scuttled out onto his kitchen steps, and stared. Then, shrugging his thin shoulders, he pattered back to his pots and pans. These foreign devils were past his understanding.

If they chose to run, helter skelter, down the valley, on a broiling hot day, that was their own concern. Probably it was some foreign-devil game, like dancing. In any event, it was no concern of Sing's. Indeed, when first Sing had seen a roomful of foreign-devil-men and girls dancing vigorously, on a hot night, his comment to a fellow-Cantonese had been:

"Why don't they make their servants do it for them?"

Klyda reached the valley-entrance, panting from fatigue, yet with pluck and resolution undimmed. As she took her first step into the labyrinth of rocky undergrowth, she heard a crashing sound just ahead of her. Halting, she leveled her pistol. Then, ashamed, she lowered it again and hid it in her shirt. For Guy Manell came puffing toward her.

"No use!" he exclaimed, disappointedly, as he gained her side. "Not a sign of him. If I'd had sense enough to go after him the instant he fired, I might have found him. But I gave him too long a start. Thirty seconds leeway in that tangle of rocks and bushes is enough for a man to lose himself forever. He's gotten clean away. Lord, what a fool I am!"

Then, suddenly realizing what her presence implied, he frowned down into her flushed face uplifted so anxiously to him.

"It was fine of you to come along and help," said he. "But you were taking a foolish risk, to no good. I told you to wait there."

"I know you did," she answered rebelliously. "But I'm disobedient, by nature. I don't take orders, like your poor submissive collie."

"That's why a good dog is a better chum than the average woman," said Guy, still vexed at his failure and at the odd twinge of joy her unexpected presence in the thicket had given him. "Dogs know when to obey."

"They obey because they know that even a man has more sense — once in a while, anyway — than a dog," flashed Klyda. "But till men get more sense than women they can't expect women to obey them, can they?"

"If they did expect it," grumbled Manell, "that's all the good it would do them, I suppose. Shall we go back? I don't give it as an order. But it's hot here. And it's cool on the porch. Besides, there's still a lot of cold water in the pitcher."

She laughed. Together they retraced their way toward the cottage. As they went, Guy saw Dawn's pitifully deserted pose on the top step of the veranda; and he snapped his fingers at the collie.

Instantly, the dog was up. At a bound he cleared the steps and came galloping to meet his master, the gray-and-white coat glistening like snow-flecked silver in the sun as he swept along the emerald meadow.

"If I'd had my wits about me," said Manell,

"I'd not have sent him back, just now. He can catch a trail and follow it like any bloodhound in a storybook. I'd have come close to laying our gold-bullet friend by the heels, with Dawn to track him. But the dog kept getting in front of me and almost upsetting me while I was running. So I —"

"Look!" interrupted Klyda, in wonder, pointing in front of her.

Chapter 5

They had just rounded the corner of the cottage, at the side of the veranda. Something yellowish-gray and shapeless was climbing the stair in a leisurely way, flowing upward rather than walking. It was at this weird object the girl pointed.

The gray creature gained the summit of the steps. It crossed to the table, and flowed up the side of that, as well. Perching itself on the summit, it reached one black little hand toward the plate of sweet crackers which Sing had brought out on the porch along with the water.

Picking up the nearest cracker, the animal smelt it in epicurean fashion. Then, leaning over, it dowsed the cracker into the water-pitcher and shook it to and fro, rinsing it carefully. At last, drawing the pulpy and dripping morsel from the water, the beast proceeded to eat the delicacy, in dainty mouthfuls, sitting on its haunches.

But by this time, Klyda's excitement had changed to reluctant mirth. She recognized the gray intruder as a huge and obese raccoon.

"It's the Reverend Wilberforce," explained Guy. "I'm sorry he's made such hash of the crackers and water. I thought he was asleep, up a tree, somewhere. Usually he is, when I want him. He's an engaging sort of pet; except that he's never around when I'd like to romp with him. And he's always around when I don't. I'll call Sing to shut him up and to clear away that mess. He —"

"But why do you call him 'the Reverend Wilberforce'?" demanded the girl, as the coon chattered indignantly at Manell's forceful removal of him from the banquet board.

"Why not?" countered Guy, setting down the disgruntled animal on the floor and rousing him to further protests by rumpling his soft fur the wrong way. "Besides, the name fits him, after a fashion. He sits up on the topmost post of the henyard and orates to the chickens by the hour, in a squealy, chuckly sort of voice. And they all stand in a silent half-circle below, with their silly heads on one side, and listen to him in solemn delight. They seem hypnotized. It reminds me, a bit, of an old steel engraving we had at home, called *The Reverend Wilberforce, Preaching to the Savages.*'"

"I see," gravely assented the girl. "But I hope his sermons to them don't deal with the sin of theft. If they do, the little cracker-thief must be an arrant hypocrite."

"If cleanliness is next to godliness," argued Guy, "it ought to atone for a few of his sins. He never eats a mouthful of anything, without washing it first. No matter whether it's a lump of ice or a bit of sugar or a live fish. And he washes his face, a dozen times a day. Once he washed it in a glass of grape jelly that Sing had set out to cool.

43

Then he tried to pat my face. Dawn went hunting, long ago, and brought him home to me — a squirming, snarling, biting month-old baby. He's lived with us ever since. I'm rather fond of him."

"I don't wonder. Except when he has been eating jelly. You're lucky to have gotten such a present from Gray Dawn."

"I'm luckier than the Reverend Wilberforce, I'm afraid. Soon or late a dog or a hunter will get him."

"Oh, no!"

"Oh yes. That's the way it goes, nearly always. Fritz Van de Water is wise. And he knows the forests and the wild things. Van de Water says when you tame a creature of the Wild, you are signing its death-warrant. He's right. You rob the animal of its natural fear of man and of its wilderness caution. So it falls easy prey to any marauding human or beast. That's why I was foolish to make a pet of the Reverend Wilberforce. Some day when he drifts away for a stroll he is due to —"

He paused. The girl's attention had wandered. Furtively, she was glancing back toward the thickets. Guy read her thoughts aright.

"Don't worry!" he soothed her. "He fired; and he missed me. That took away his nerve. (It always does; so a gunman told me.) Then I chased him. And he's probably running yet. There's nothing more to fear from him. Come up in the shade and sit down. Please don't be frightened.

The danger is past. For today, anyhow."

He stooped and scanned the sunlit surface of the porch for the gold bullet he had dropped there when he ran in pursuit of the unseen marksman.

"Did you happen to pick up that blob of gold, after I was gone?" he asked Klyda.

"No," she said. "I never thought of it again. I saw you toss it down there when you started off. After that I was too busy, looking after you, and then following you, to notice it. What's become of it?"

"It's gone," he made answer, bewilderedly. "And it didn't roll off the porch, either. It was as flat as a wafer, and its edges were irregular. It couldn't have rolled or bounced. I saw it fall and lie there. Why, even the tiny spatters are gone!"

"Perhaps your Chinaman —"

"Sing? The Chinks aren't saints. But I never heard of one of them that would steal from his boss. A Chink house servant is an honest house servant. A dozen times Sing has brought me coins and the like, that I've dropped and that he found. No, we can count him out. And — and nobody else can have been here, in the few minutes we've been gone. Dawn wouldn't have let anyone up on the porch."

"Perhaps the Reverend Wilberforce ate it," she suggested, flippantly, to mask an unbidden sensation of creepiness that stole over her at the unexplainable vanishing of the even more unexplainable bullet.

"Sweet crackers are more in his line than gold," said Manell. "I know the Reverend Wilberforce fairly well; including all his many sins. But he would never be fool enough to gobble a piece of metal. Especially when there are crackers within reach. He's crazy about sweet crackers. It was the smell of them that brought him here from whatever place he was napping. No, we can leave out the Reverend Wilberforce. The fact remains that the golden bullet is gone. It *couldn't* have gone. But it has."

Chapter 6

As his eyes met Klyda's a tinge of her own awed amazement was in his glance. Before either of them could speak, a voice hailed them, from the bridge beyond. They turned nervously, in answer to the hail.

There, coming toward them from the bridge, was a thick-set man of perhaps fifty, upstanding and powerful in spite of his grizzling hair and lined face. He was dressed in the same general type of outing clothes as Klyda's.

"It's Dad!" announced the girl, starting across the meadow to meet the newcomer. "He must have come to the bridge and seen me here. And I'd forgotten all about meeting him!"

She hurried on, Manell following more slowly. Guy could have forgiven Saul Graeme for delaying his return to the meeting place for another half hour or even another half day. Now he was aware of positive annoyance that the father should have broken in on his strange acquaintance with Klyda.

Yet, hospitably, he advanced to meet his new guest. He came within earshot just as Klyda was recounting hastily the adventures of the morning. So absorbed was she in telling her narrative and so wonderingly interested was Saul Graeme in listening to it that Guy did not break in upon her recital until she started to speak of his own courage in charging, unarmed, after his invisible enemy. Then, embarrassed, he intruded himself on the attention of the dumbfoundedly listening man.

Hand outstretched, he said:

"I'm a neighbor of yours, Mr. Graeme. And I'm going to take advantage of that to insist that you and Miss Graeme stay to lunch with me, today. She must be tired. So must you. It's more than a mile to your ranch. Sing will have lunch ready in another ten minutes. You must stay."

Waving aside their perfunctory excuses, he carried his point.

"I suppose we ought to say 'No,' " said Klyda, as the three started back toward the house. "And I feel it's an imposition. But I've been dreading, for an hour, to get that cranky stove of ours to working, and then to cook lunch, in all this heat. You're not a mere neighbor, Mr. Manell. You're a benefactor."

"No," denied Guy, "I'm a beneficiary. Besides —"

"And Dad has one of his torture-headaches, too," she went on. "At least he's starting to have. I can always tell, by that craggy look at the corner of his eyes. If he had to tramp another mile in the sun and then sit around in a hot shack while lunch was getting ready, he —"

"Nonsense!" broke in Graeme. "This sun is enough to give anyone a headache. Mine isn't worth speaking of. You mustn't let this little girl give you the idea I'm a mollycoddle or a hypo-chondriac, Mr. Manell. I'm as strong as a team of oxen. But she tries to make a baby of me."

Lightly as Graeme spoke, his host could see the "craggy look" about his eyes and the droop of repressed pain around his mouth corners. And Guy knew by experience the crippling effects of a sick headache.

"Sit here in the shade," he bade his guests. "It's cooler than indoors. I'll go and tell Sing to hurry our lunch. We can eat out in the breeze. I always do, when I'm alone. I'll take the Reverend Wilberforce along, and tie him up. His table manners are cleanly but unconventional. Almost primitive. As an encourager of any appetite, except his own, he's not to be recommended. There are more congenial table-companions than he is. Come along, Rev.!"

He tucked the snarlingly unwilling raccoon under his arm, and went indoors. Depositing the Reverend Wilberforce in a backsteps coop and chaining him there, he proceeded to make Sing miserable by ordering the most elaborate lun-cheon his mind could rise to or that the very frugal larder could encompass. Enjoining haste on the gloomy Chinaman and stopping to gather a handful of golden dooryard poppies for the table, he returned to his guests.

He found Saul Graeme leaning back in the big rocker, eyes shut, mighty body relaxed; while Klyda's white little fingers smoothed his lionlike head.

49

At sound of his host's return the man pushed gently aside the caressing fingers and got to his feet. There was a furtively troubled air about him; or so it seemed to Guy.

"My daughter has a wonderfully magnetic touch, Mr. Manell," he said, shamefacedly. "And she loves to coddle me. I ought not to let her do it. But — well — somehow, I like it. By the way, she has been telling me about that golden bullet and its disappearing. How do you account for such an impossible thing?"

"Only by agreeing that it was an 'impossible thing,'" said Guy. "Impossible things can't be accounted for. If I'd been here alone, I'd never have dared ask anyone to believe such a yarn. But we both saw it."

"You're sure it was gold?" asked Graeme, curiously.

"Yes. As a matter of fact, I happen to know a little about such things. I was educated at the Columbia School of Mines. Metallurgy was almost the one subject I never flunked in. During sophomore vacation (I was dropped in junior year) I worked in an assay office. I made a specialty of gold. It was my hobby."

"But —"

"But this bullet was twenty-four carat virgin gold; rough-smelted. 'Flour gold,' at that. One of the finest — if not the very finest — grades of gold. It almost seems as if someone had taken such raw gold and melted it down and run it into a bullet-mold. It's a sure thing there aren't

50

enough gold bullets made, in all the world, to justify buying a machine to make them with. And they're not cast at any ammunition factory."

"But that's —"

"No, the bullet that grazed me must have been made especially, and then fitted into a cartridge that the leaden ball had been taken out of. I should feel honored at so much wealth and the time and bother being wasted on me. No wonder the precious bullet was disgusted, and vanished!"

"It isn't a joke!" rebuked Klyda, shuddering. "And you're making a joke of it, just to keep us from worrying. Can't you get the State Police to —"

"To follow up a man who shoots gold bullets and then gets them back by magic?" suggested Graeme. "Why, dear, Mr. Manell would probably be sent to an asylum for telling the police such a tale. He —"

"But it's the truth!" protested the girl. "We both saw —"

"Truth isn't merely stranger than fiction," said Guy. "From police standards, it's more unusual. Your father is right. I couldn't carry such a story to the police, even if I wanted to. And I don't want to. The same man is likely to try again, in some other form. Now that I'm on my guard, I'll back my own chances of catching him without bawling for the police."

Fearing lest his assurance be taken for

boasting, he changed the subject abruptly.

"The odd part of it is," he resumed, "that this is not a gold region. It never was. There has never been gold, to any extent, in this part of California, nor within many miles of here. So how did my murderous friend get hold of flour gold and — ?"

He shrugged his shoulders and finished:

"At that, it may have been some gold ornament melted down, and not the raw gold. Only, almost no ornaments are made of twenty-four carat gold. Like coins, they have a big percentage of alloy, to harden them. But this bullet was soft enough for my fingernail to dent it."

The arrival of Sing interrupted him. The Chinaman proceeded dismally to set the table for luncheon. When he had returned to the kitchen for the soup, and the three were seating themselves, Saul Graeme said, hesitantly:

"Something happened, this morning, that I was ashamed to speak about, because I thought it might have been just an accident. I still think so. But it was queer."

He turned to his daughter.

"I drew as blank on my side of the slope as you did," said he. "At least, in all but one place. I found a series of rock-faults that gave me climbing hold. They were on the side of the mountain beyond that deep groove. I started up them, thinking I could get to the ledge above, that way, more easily than by going all the distance around to the groove. There were clumps of green, on that part of the ledge. I thought maybe they marked a rock-spring."

"They may," assented Guy. "I've thought of looking. I've only explored the other side of the ledge. It breaks off, between the two sides, you know, and leaves a sheer perpendicular wall. . . . Go ahead. I didn't mean to interrupt you."

"I got perhaps a third of the way up," pursued Graeme, "when a stone, the size of my fist, came bouncing down at me from nowhere at all. It missed me by a few inches. And it gave me a scare. If it had tapped me on the head, I'd have gone down to the bottom of the climb, without ever knowing what killed me. Or it might have smashed my arm or hand and left me helpless to get up or down."

His daughter's fingers touched his, unobtrusively, in a quick gesture of sympathy. Her face blanched a trifle.

"Of course, it was only an accident," she said. "But it might —"

"That's what I thought," replied her father. "I stopped a minute, to think it over. Then I remembered that there probably are lots of loose stones lying on the ledges of all high mountains; and that gusts of wind or the feet of wild animals can easily send them toppling over. It wasn't likely to happen again. So I went on with my climb."

He paused, hesitant, then said:

"About two minutes later, down hurtled another stone, twice as big as the first. It didn't

53

bounce along the side of the mountain, but dropped clean. And I could feel the wind of it, as it whizzed by me. You'll laugh at me. But those two happenings got on my nerves. I began to climb down. Just as I got to the bottom and took off my hat to wipe my forehead, a third stone fell."

"No!" exclaimed Klyda.

"It missed me," said Graeme. "But it got my hat. It went through the tough felt as it would have gone through paper. It knocked the hat out of my hand; and the jerk of it jarred my arm to the elbow. This time I wasn't frightened. I was good and mad. Besides, I was on old terra firma again. I ran back to where I could see the whole side of the mountain, all the way up to the ledge."

"Was there — ?"

"Not a sign of anyone, nor of any beast or bird. I calmed down, and figured (as I still figure) that it was just a coincidence. Probably fifty stones a day tumble from those windy ledges. I just happened to be in the path of three of them. But I had the sensation that someone was throwing rocks at me; and it made me lose my temper."

"Did you notice if there were many loose stones lying on the ground below the ledge?" asked Klyda. "I mean at the place where you climbed?"

"No," said Graeme, "there weren't. I — I looked. Of course it was just chance. Now that I've put the story into words, I see it must have been chance. But one gets jumpy, alone out there, halfway between heaven and earth. It was foolish of me to mention it at all. . . . Will you forgive me for saying this is the best soup I have tasted since I left the East?"

"Thanks so much for the fulsome compliment to my cooking!" laughed Klyda.

Yet under her forced laugh, Guy could see her father's adventure had shaken her, coming as it did on the top of her own experiences of the morning.

"One thing is settled," decreed Graeme, presently. "Hereafter, I do my water-hunting alone, daughter. And you'll stay at home or in some other civilized place. I'm not going to have you meeting burlap-masked men again, in the wilds, or risking stones dropping on that pretty head of yours. Remember! Today's visit to Grudge Mountain was your last."

"And let you go there all alone to — ?"

"Kid," said Graeme, "I'm fifty years old, this month. For nearly thirty of those fifty years I had to slink through life without your invaluable protection. I'll stagger along without it for a while longer, when it comes to exploring Grudge Mountain for water. You can stay at the shack and take lessons in trying to make such soup as this. It'll be more of a service to me than to have you a nervous wreck on my hands, from wilderness adventures. Remember, you've said a last good-by to Grudge Mountain!"

Chapter 7

Two hours later, Guy Manell turned his rattling little car into the stable garage, back of his cottage; after taking Klyda and Graeme to their ranch. This final act of neighborliness he had insisted on performing, despite the protests of his guests, who declared they were well able to walk home.

But even the luncheon and the hour of rest had not wiped the pain-lines from Saul's face. Indeed, he confessed reluctantly that his sick headache was steadily growing worse. Klyda, too, was manifestly tired from her long walk in the sun. And she was shaken by her adventures. So neither of them offered very earnest objections to Manell's plan.

Guy frowned annoyedly now, as he recalled the cheerless look of the Graemes' new abode, and realized that a girl like Klyda must rough it in such a place.

He recalled the barren stony hillside, brush-and-weed-choked, where Saul contemplated planting his raisin vineyard; this, after a drag of steel rails and much subsequent plowing and harrowing should have cleared the cluttered land, and irrigation laterals should have been dug; and, most important of all, water discovered.

He recalled the miserable shack, half-lean-to,

half-tent, which served the two as a temporary home until a house could be built, and the ill-drawing stove and the makeshift furniture and the general air of squalor. Not even the scrupulous neatness and brightly clean aspect of everything in the shack — not even the big jars of brilliant lupine and poppies and misty wild lilac on tables and on window shelves — could efface that slum aspect.

Manell hated to think of so dainty and highbred a girl striving to make a real home out of such unpromising material, and slaving to keep it neat and cosy. He began to loathe Saul Graeme for allowing his delicately nurtured daughter to undergo these hardships. Nor had he any great faith in Graeme's ability to make a success at grape-growing. Apart from the contents of his sheaf of government pamphlets, Saul's information and experience along such lines appeared to be most rudimentary.

Guy set him down as one of the countless visionary cranks who drift to the Far West because they cannot make good in the East, and who count on the richness of that Land of Promise to make up to them for their own lack of thrift and of mental equipment. He pitied Klyda more and more for having such a father, even while he admired her for her staunch loyalty toward the dreamy old giant who had brought her out into this wilderness. To his own annoyed surprise, Guy found it hard and harder to keep her out of his mind.

It was too late in the day to pick up his routine labors. Nor did he feel like blotting out the memories of the morning and noontide by going back to work. Sing was setting off to the nearest town, Santa Dereta, with a basket under his arm, to repair the inroads of the lunchers by laying in a new stock of provisions. Guy sought to interest himself in pottering about the grounds at various petty chores. Somehow he could not throw aside an odd feeling of restlessness.

At last he gave up. On the rare times when he was depressed or otherwise ill at ease, a brisk tramp through the foothills served always as a tonic to him. Whistling now to Gray Dawn, he started aimlessly toward the valley-entrance, the big silver collie dancing happily along in front.

Manell excused himself for the waste of time by pretending he wanted another appraising look at the ground over which his assailant must have retreated. There might be some clue, on bush or rock.

There was no such clue. Half an hour's swinging stride had brought Guy far beyond the valley-mouth and up along the craggy ring of hills which encircled the base of Grudge Mountain.

The setting sun struck in level rays athwart the grim mountainside, tinging its harsh gray with a blood-red light, though the lower foothills were in dusk. Manell could see above him the "groove" furrowing its steep upward way to the higher and larger of the cliffside's two ledges —

the wooded groove he was planning to explore again in quest of water.

Then, shoulder-high amid the strewn foothill rocks, he came to a standstill. His wandering eye had passed on from the groove to the wide ledge at its upper end. The vivid red light of sunset brought the ledge into unnaturally clear relief, even to the slightest inequalities of its surface.

There, on its brink, mercilessly outlined by the sunset, were two figures. From where Guy stood, there was no mistaking them; as he halted he himself was unseen amid the shadows and the high rocks of the lower ground.

The two people on the higher ledge were Klyda Graeme and her father. And Klyda had told him she was going to make Saul go to bed until his headache should be cured. She had said she herself was too tired to get supper, until an hour's nap could brace her for a bout with the smoky stove!

They had hurried home early from Friendly Valley, on this dual plea of illness and of overfatigue. Yet here they both were, miles from their shack, on a ledge which would take the strength and energy of an unwearied athlete to attain!

They were not standing idle. They were poring over something which Saul held in front of him, something whose nature the man below could not make out.

"Why did they lie to me?" blithered Guy, to Gray Dawn, speaking to his dog as does many a lonely man, as if the collie were a fellow-human. "There's no law against their being up on that ledge. Why did they pretend they were tuckered out and sick? Why did they sneak up there as soon as they could get out of my way? They broke bread with me — and then they lied to me! Why? Tell me that, Dawn! And — and I'd have sworn she was the squarest girl God ever made. Why, her eyes made me feel as if — as if I were in church! And she lied to me, Dawn!"

Dawn wiggled, self-consciously, eyes sparkling, at the reiterations of his name; and he waved his plumed tail in flattering interest.

With a grunt that had more of pain in it than of mere disillusion, Manell snapped his fingers to his expectantly waiting collie, and turned homeward. Once only did he glance back. The two figures were no longer in sight. Angry with himself for the queer hurt at his heart, Manell plodded glumly toward his cottage in its sweet setting of lush grass and trees and blossoms.

"Gray Dawn," he said, "back home at Pompton Lakes, acres of soft green grass are a platitude. Up here, they are a throbbing epigram."

Sing had not yet returned from Santa Dereta. Yet the house was not silent. From the kitchen stoop came the unceasing sound of a cross voice scolding. The muttering voice was wordless. Guy recognized it as the Reverend Wilberforce's. He remembered now that he had chained the raccoon to his coop and had forgotten to loose him. At such times, the Reverend Wilberforce was wont to sleep away philosophically his hours of captivity. He had an infinite genius for slumber. Never before had he resented confinement; never in this noisily wrathful style.

Supposing the coon had become enmeshed somehow with his chain and was trying to scold himself out of the tangle, Guy went around to investigate.

No, the Reverend Wilberforce was not tangled in his chain. He was sitting on his hind legs, waving his black hands threateningly at something that flapped in the breeze from the kitchen's screen door, just beyond his reach.

It was a large sheet of cheap and coarse brown paper, such as meat sometimes is wrapped in. But nothing had been wrapped in this paper. There was not a single crease nor crumple in its 20-by-20-inch surface. The sunset breeze was making it wag and crackle. This manifestation, apparently, had roused the displeasure of the Reverend Wilberforce; or else the sheet had struck him as a desirable plaything.

Guy took the wide brownish paper from the rusty pin wherewith it was skewered to the screen door. Across its surface was scrawled laboriously in a reddish fluid that seemed too thick for ink:

"The suner yu git out of heer the loanger yu wil liv. This is the 1st warrning. It won't be reel helthfull for yu to wate for the next (2d) one."

Chapter 8

The square of crackling brown paper fell, un-
heeded, from Guy's fingers. With furrowed brow
he was staring into space, across the rich little
valley, up toward the distant bulk of Grudge
Mountain.

The warning did not frighten him. It did not
even make him angry. Its only immediate effect
was to puzzle him and to daze him.

His three-year sojourn in this green cup of the
Sierras had been marked by good fellowship and
peace with his few neighbors. They were easygoing and likable and industrious. He had gotten
on well with all sorts and conditions of folk, from
fellow-ranchers to such of the itinerant "bindle
stiffs" as occasionally he had hired.

He had minded his own business. He had lent
a helping hand, when occasion called. He had
made no enemies, that he knew of. Nor was this
industrial corner of the state — like the Bakersfield region — the scene of neighborhood feuds
and hates, nor of I.W.W. venom.

Yet, here, he had received a most dramatic, if
carefully ill-spelt, warning to depart. He knew of
no practical jokers in the neighborhood. Nor, for
the mere sake of a joke, would anyone have been
likely to risk a flaming attack from Gray Dawn

nor detection by one of Guy's ranchworkers, by stealing up to the cottage and affixing such a notice to the door.

This morning, he had been shot at. By an impossible 24-carat gold bullet, at that. This evening he was warned, anonymously, to get out. Even if the warning were a joke, the shot was not. Taken together, they were mystifying enough to cause the pucker on his smooth forehead. The same enemy does not shoot, usually, and then warn. Were there two people — or two sets of people — who had declared war on him? And why should anyone do such a silly thing?

The paper had not been there when Sing set out for Santa Dereta on his provision trip. For Guy had passed from the house by way of the kitchen door; and nothing had been pinned on the screen at that time. No, it had been done during his own walk to the foot of Grudge Mountain and back. It had been done perhaps at the very minute when he had been staring dumbfoundedly up at Saul Graeme and Klyda, on the ledge above him.

Shaking off his daze, Manell stooped to pick up the sheet of brown paper, to reread it and to determine what might be the sticky reddish liquid with which its misspelt words were scrawled.

But he was too late.

The paper had fallen to the adobe floor directly in front of the Reverend Wilberforce's coop. The raccoon was more fortunate than are most humans. For the thing he had been scolding for and trying in vain to reach, had tumbled at his very feet. The Reverend Wilberforce had gathered it up into his absurdly human little black hands; and he had crumpled it into a ball. Then he seemed to decide that it was good to eat. And, as in the case of everything eatable, he first thrust it into the waterpail beside his coop; sloshing it vigorously back and forth.

He was drawing it loose from its bath, when Guy Manell bent to look at it. Guy rescued the sodden pulp from the Reverend Wilberforce's indignantly resisting grasp. But it was undecipherable, now. It was nothing but a wad of water-rotted fibre with no resemblance to a sheet of paper — to say nothing of a written page.

The raccoon's passion for cleanliness had spoiled Guy's one chance of studying the anonymous warning and of trying to glean from it some faint clue to its author. The man shrugged his broad shoulders in philosophic resignation, saying, as he went indoors:

"Rev., if you'd spent as much time learning to talk as learning to wash things, you could spill the whole mystery to me. He must have leaned across you, to pin that to the screen. It's a pity all animals can't talk — and that all humans can."

He was breakfasting on the veranda, early next morning, after a night of little sleep and of much perplexed thought, when two people appeared on the road, beside the bridge.

Even before they stepped down into the meadow and began to approach the porch — even before Gray Dawn jumped up from beside his master's chair to run forward to meet them, with stippled ears flattened back and with plumed brush hysterically awag — Guy recognized his early visitors as Klyda Graeme and her father.

He did not move, nor did he give sign of seeing them. Placidly he went on eating — or pretending to eat. Though he had been without appetite, his food now took on a taste of ashes. He was furious at himself for the ridiculous way his heart had jolted at bare sight of the girl whom he had spent the whole night in learning to despise. He was far less displeased at the flood of righteous anger which encompassed him.

These were people whom he had befriended, and who had rewarded him by lies — by clumsy and needless deceit. He felt affronted at their second visit; and he was hard put to it to school himself to meet them civilly.

Now, Klyda's light footfall was on the bottom step of the porch. The voice of her father was hailing him. No longer could he assume ignorance of their presence. To himself, Guy was saying, for the sixtieth time since yesterday:

"He said she must never go near Grudge Mountain again. Told her so, at this very table. Three hours afterward she was on the ledge there; and he was with her. Told me they were worn out and that he was going to bed to sleep off his sick headache. And the second they got rid of me, they started for Grudge Mountain. The babyish liars!"

But while he was inwardly railing at them, Manell was getting to his feet and going to the head of the steps to greet his guests. His face was cold, as was his stiff "Good Morning." He seemed not to see the hand Saul was thrusting at him in bluff friendliness. But he avoided overt rudeness — or he flattered himself that he did.

It was Klyda who noted first the utter change in his manner since the day before. She looked at him in hurt wonder. He evaded meeting her big eyes. Curtly he asked her father if the two had eaten. This was the sacrosanct formula wherewith all the region's folk hailed visitors.

"Yes," responded Saul in booming good fellowship. "We've had breakfast. Such as it was. We're early birds. We had breakfast before sunrise. You see, neither of us did much sleeping. That's why we've dropped in on you so early. We're bothered about something. You're the only acquaintance we have, hereabouts. We want to ask your advice."

Guy nodded, noncommittally, still avoiding Klyda's eyes.

"Won't you sit down?" he asked, coldly.

For answer, Saul Graeme took from his pocket a bulky brown object. This he proceeded to unfold, talking as he did so.

"Here is something we found pinned to the tent-flap of our lean-to," said he. "What do you

66

make of it, Mr. Manell?"

He had finished unfolding the thing and handed it to Guy. It was a 20-by-20 sheet of coarse brown paper. On it, in reddish letters, were scrawled the identical words of warning which Guy himself had found attached to his kitchen door-screen:

"The suner yu git out of heer the loanger yu wil liv. This is the 1st warrning. It won't be reel helthfull for yu to wate for the next (2d) one."

For an instant Manell was startled out of his icy reserve. He gaped from the paper to Saul and then to Klyda.

The hurt look was still in the girl's great dark eyes. But her voice was level and calm as she said:

"Do you think this was meant as a joke, Mr. Manell? It can't be anything else. We have no enemies, anywhere. Least of all here, where we are strangers. And surely nobody can want to scare us off, for the sake of getting our land. It isn't good enough for that. What do you make of — ?"

"I don't know," said Guy, dully. He forbore, on sudden impulse, to say he had received a like warning.

"We don't know whether to believe it is genuine or to take it as a hoax," put in Saul, worriedly. "That's why I suggested we come over and ask your opinion. I was for coming over the minute we found it. But you know how done up and sick I was. So we waited till —"

"When did you find it?" interposed Manell.

67

"When we got back from —" began Klyda; then she checked herself, flushing to the roots of her hair.

"Yes," her father caught her up, smoothly, "we found it when we got up from our nap. After you left us, at the shack, yesterday, it was so hot indoors that we decided to rest under the clump of dwarf pines, about a hundred yards from the house; there the breeze could blow over us. My head was pretty bad. And the long walk and your good luncheon — the inspired soup, perhaps — had made Klyda sleepy, too. We dozed most of the afternoon. Then I woke up. I started indoors, to find my tobacco pouch. On the tent-flap was pinned this — this square of brown paper, with its blood-colored scribble, warning us to leave. Someone must have tiptoed up and pinned it there while we were asleep."

Guy no longer sought to elude Klyda's gaze. He had kept his eyes fixed quietly upon her, throughout her father's elaborate glib narrative. She had fidgeted under his look, getting redder and redder, and at last lowering her own lids.

"About what time was that?" Manell asked Graeme, his glance still full upon the girl.

"I can tell you exactly," said the older man. "Because I looked at my watch when I woke up, to see how long I had been asleep. And I went directly across to the shack, not a minute later. It was eighteen minutes past five."

This time, Klyda flinched, perceptibly. She lifted her eyes again to Guy's. In their dark

68

depths, now, there was a dumb appeal and something akin to shame.

"Eighteen minutes past five?" mused Guy, to himself. "And I saw you both, on Grudge Mountain ledge, at about five-thirty. You must have traveled at a pretty pace, to cover all those miles of broken ground, on foot, and then work your way up that steep groove — in twelve minutes!"

Aloud, he said, choking back his growing contempt as best he could:

"I'm afraid I can't advise you. I'm a plain Kern County rancher. I travel a rather narrow and old-fashioned line of simplicity. I can't summon enough imagination to tell a plausible lie, to say nothing of solving anonymous-letter mysteries. It may be genuine. Or it may be a fake. I'm sorry I can't help you decide which."

His tone held a distinctly unfriendly note which even Saul Graeme could not ignore. The older man peered surprisedly at his host, then he looked at his daughter, as though asking her the meaning of this baffling change of manner in the host who yesterday had been so cordial with them.

For answer Klyda arose from the porch edge, where she had seated herself with Gray Dawn cuddling affectionately against her side.

"Joke or earnest," she said calmly, "we are going to treat it the way all anonymous letters should be treated. We are going to pay no attention to it. We have done nothing wrong. Nobody has the right to harm us. I don't believe anyone will. Come, Dad! We are keeping Mr. Manell from his breakfast. You'll forgive us, Mr. Manell, for breaking in on you?"

Guy tried to say something conventionally polite. But the words jammed in his throat. He bowed, and got up from his chair. Saul continued to stare at him, bewildered at the odd change of manner.

"Anything new about the golden bullet mystery?" asked Saul, to break the awkward pause.

"No," said Manell, shortly.

With another wondering look at his daughter, as though asking her anew to explain their host's new coldness, Graeme got up and followed Klyda down the steps.

Guy stood watching them as they recrossed the meadow and gained the bridge and the road. He could have sworn there were tears in the girl's big eyes as she had turned hastily away.

The thought stung him, like a whiplash. Try as he would, he could not muster his earlier indignant disgust at her deception. Whenever he tried to, the realization of her falsehood was blotted out by a memory of tear-filled eyes in an unhappy little face — the face of a grieving child.

Chapter 9

Leaving his breakfast unfinished, Guy went in quest of his foreman, and gave his orders for the day. Then, after a hasty inspection of his vineyards and his workers, he whistled to Gray Dawn and started afresh for Grudge Mountain.

In his present mood, he wanted to be away from everyone until he should have hit upon some solution of the tangle that perplexed him or until he could argue his turbulent heart back to normal. Moreover, he had promised himself a day up there, to explore for water. Yesterday, the meeting with Klyda Graeme, on the trail, had wrecked his plans. Now, he resolved to go on with the expedition.

But his craving to be alone was not to be gratified so easily. As he left the cottage behind him and made for the valley-mouth, a man came down from the road and hailed him.

Guy turned about, to confront one of his workers, Jenner by name, who had not turned up that morning.

Jenner was of the class locally known as "bindle stiffs." These are itinerant day-laborers, as a rule. Sometimes the term is applied to tramps as well. With no luggage except what can be strapped in their shoulder-blankets, they wander through California on foot, picking up odd jobs and then drifting on when the fancy strikes them. "Bindle" is a corruption of "bundle" or of "blanket."

In the 1920's, a goodly number of these stiffs, who professed loud admiration for the precepts of the I.W.W., were rounded up, in a Kern County bull-pen; and were subjected to hideous torture by having cool water from the fire-hose sprayed on them until they were washed nearly clean. After which they were invited most cordially to leave the town and the county. They did so — the terrors of fresh water prevailing, where threats of jail martyrdom (and of free board and lodging) had been received with jeers.

This particular bindle stiff had been working for Guy, during the past five months. He seemed one of the best of his kind. He was moderately honest (at least, in the absence of temptation), and industrious enough while the foreman's eye or Manell's was upon him.

He was merely an unskilled laborer, of the sort who once received a bare dollar a day in wage. Just after the World War, the pay of even an unskilled bindle stiff soared for a while to something above five dollars, then simmered to somewhere from three-fifty to four dollars a day.

Ranchers fumed. But pay that much they must, or go without labor. They fumed impotently — all except the Japs and members of one or two other foreign races which have made California their Mecca. These foreigners impress the women and children of their own families into service on their farms, working them and themselves early and late and thus saving wages and often waxing rich. The more especially as they live and thrive on food which an American would gag at.

"Morning, Boss!" called Jenner, as he came within earshot. "I want to speak to you a minute."

"Why didn't you choose a minute, a couple of hours ago?" asked Manell. "You were due on the job then. Been in town to wire orders to your broker or only just to try out a new limousine?"

The bindle stiff grinned, dutifully, at his employer's dull effort at humor. But at once his face grew grave, even troubled. And now Guy saw the man was wearing his dirty blanket, knapsack-fashion, as if for the road.

"What's the blanket for?" he demanded.

"That's what I wanted to speak to you about," said Jenner. "Boss, I'm through. I want my time."

He spoke defiantly. But his eyes were downcast; and one of his broganed feet was tracing patterns in the grass. Not thus as a rule do bindle stiffs behave when they announce airily their intention to move on. Guy was puzzled.

"Better job, up the line?" he asked.

"Nope," was the sullen answer. "Maybe I'll find something. Maybe I won't. I'll see how the luck runs."

"Feet itching, hey?"

"Nope," still more sullenly. "I ain't bit by the roadbug, this time. I was lotting on staying out the year."

"The grub's rotten, I suppose," hazarded Guy, his curiosity aroused, "and the foreman's crowding you too hard and keeping you awake all day. Too bad about you!"

"Grub's rotten, every place," grunted Jenner. "No worse here than other places. Work's bad everywhere, too; and foremen is all swine. Your ranch ain't worse'n the rest, though."

"Then, why in blazes are you clearing out?"

"I'm going," evaded Jenner. "Going. That's all. Just going."

Something in his furtive and worried manner hit Manell as increasingly peculiar. Guy went on with his queries, but less directly.

"I'm short-handed," said he. "You know that. And the rush season is just about setting in. You're leaving me flat. Why?"

"I'm sorry I got to," said Jenner, shuffling from foot to foot. "You ain't a bad boss to work for. Not as bosses go. You average up, pretty fair. I'm sorry I got to leave you short-handed. But there's no good in my singing a song about it, is there? I want my time."

"Let's see," resumed Manell, "you're getting $3.75, aren't you? How about $4.25?"

"Nothing doing, Boss," returned Jenner, yet with visible regret.

"An even $6 a day?" suggested Guy.

He knew full well he would not pay the man

74

such an absurd sum. But he was anxious to get at the bottom of the queer situation. It is well, on a ranch, to trace the cause of any unwonted labor-dissatisfaction.

"How about that? Stay for six dollars a day?"

Jenner heaved a ponderous sigh of renunciation. Then he shook his head; the worried look crept again into his tanned face.

"Nope," said he.

"See here!" insisted Manell, his patience at an end. "If you want your time, you'll tell me what's the matter. Oh yes, I know you can collect it by law. But it'll take you a year to do it. Come across. What's the matter with you?"

Jenner cast a frightened glance behind him.

"There's things going on here!" he mumbled. "Things I don't like. Things that's — that's funny! I'm not staying on, no longer."

"If there's anything out of the way," scoffed Manell, though vaguely impressed by the bindle stiff's manner, "I must get after the foreman for not telling me. He —"

"He don't know nothing about it," answered Jenner. "Nor yet the rest of 'em don't. If they did, there'd be a gen'r'l walkout. There will be, too, when they know. I ain't blabbed. But neither I ain't staying. I ain't blabbed, because I don't hone to be laughed at. I ain't staying, because I don't hone for that kind of trouble. If you want to hold my pay out on me, I'm going, just the same."

There was a quality in his words and voice that

Guy thought he recognized as the unbreakable stubbornness bred of very genuine fear. He saw he could get nothing out of this man. Whether or no his dread of peril were justified, there could be no mistaking the reality of the dread.

Manell drew out a slip of paper, scribbled on it the words: "Give Jenner his time," initialed it and handed it to the bindle stiff.

"Take that to the foreman," said he.

Jenner grasped the pay slip with a grunt of genuine relief. As Guy continued his walk, the man called waveringly after him:

"I'm thanking you, Boss. And I'm sorry to walk out on you like this."

Then, lowering his voice, he added, cryptically:

"If you'll take my tip, you'll walk out, yourself. The Trouble-Wagon is backing up to this ranch of yours."

Guy turned sharply about to demand the meaning of this veiled admonition. But already Jenner had set off at a shambling run, in search of the ranch's foreman and of his pay. Nor did he look back nor slacken his pace, as Manell shouted to him to stop.

"Twenty-four-carat gold bullet fired at me," grumbled Guy as he took up his interrupted walk; "then an elaborately illiterate warning pinned to my door; then Jenner croaking misfortune like an eighteenth-century melodrama ghost! What in blue blazes is the answer?"

His mind would not stay on the triple theme

long enough to set in array any of its few known facts. For almost instantly he found his thoughts straying miserably to Klyda Graeme and to the web of petty deceit wherein she had meshed herself. He was sorry he had behaved so ungraciously to her, that morning; though he could feel no regret at snubbing her smoothly mendacious father. He felt as though he had spoken brutally to a child. Try as he would he could not keep hot his resentment toward her. He fell to visualizing her little face with its big honest eyes, and trying to reconcile it with her words and actions.

On through the foothills he went; Gray Dawn capering ahead of him, or pausing to investigate holes of ground-squirrels, or bolting madly in vain pursuit of a jack-rabbit. But as they came to the foot of the groove, the collie ceased from these morning pastimes and breasted the rise alongside his master.

The groove was perhaps fifteen feet wide, and running down to an acute-angle apex in the center. Here earth had collected. Here, too, the tangle of creosote-laden greasewood and the rank-smelling red-stemmed manzanita bushes made progress slow. But they also made progress possible, by means of the foothold and handhold they gave to a climber.

The cleft ran obliquely upward to the higher of the two ledges on that side of the mountain — a ledge perhaps a hundred yards above the mountain foot and seventy yards above its smaller fellow-ledge. The two ledges, with an occasional break, wound in varying widths around the irregular side of the peak, like balconies around a campanile.

Upward toiled Manell, the dog scrambling along at his side. The man was a trained athlete and a trained climber as well; though the two qualities go together less often than most people realize. Quietly and skillfully as he made his way, the dry wood of the bushes crackled noisily under his feet and twigs snapped at the touch of his hands. Underfoot, a pebble or two and stray bits of dirt rumbled down the troughlike groove behind him.

The dog, on the contrary, was all but noiseless, out here in the wild places. It was as though his wolf-ancestry came to his help in slipping silently and easily along the choked ascent.

Presently they came to a pinch in the side-rocks — a passage so narrow that the man had to squeeze his way through it. Gray Dawn dropped back to let Manell precede him.

Here, more clearly, Guy noted what had been visible all along the climb. Namely, new-broken branches and new-disturbed loam in the leafy footing. Recently, this groove had been climbed. Even had he not seen Graeme and Klyda the day before, on the upper ledge, Manell would have realized this.

At sign of the passage of the two, his resentment flared afresh. But just then he needed all his energies, mental as well as physical, to negotiate the toughest bit of the ascent. The groove not only narrowed, for some six or eight yards, but an outcropping of rock and of undergrowth in the point of its angle forced the climber to get down on all fours for a yard or so, and wriggle his way along.

His head penetrated some high-growing grass tufts, midway in this crawl, scarce eighteen inches above ground, as he twisted his way forward. In another foot or two he would be able to stand upright once more.

Then, holding the same awkward crawling posture, he stopped short, his body becoming as moveless as the mountain itself. From the midst of the grass tufts, almost on a level with his face and not two feet in front of him, came the vibrantly unmistakable whir-r-r-r of a rattlesnake.

Nobody who once has heard the piercing buzz of the "side-winder" rattlesnake of the upper Sierras needs be warned a second time as to the nature of the foe menacing him. From the thickest of the grass sounded this fierce threat, apparently from a spot on which Guy had been about to place his extended hand, to pull himself forward and upward.

Unseen, through the dense tangle of dry grass and leafage, the serpent was nonetheless sounding its angry defiance; the fair warning which — alone of all the viper tribe — it almost always gives before striking.

There was but one chance. Guy took that chance.

Moveless as a corpse he crouched there; resisting the mad impulse to shrink back or otherwise to evade the mortal peril. This was not his first experience with the deadly "side-winder," — the fat and dirty-hued snake, so much thicker and shorter and less spectacular than its diamond-back cousin of the Florida pine-barrens. He knew the snake was roused and meant to strike. He knew the first stir on his own part would be the certain signal for the ugly three-cornered head to dart forward with incalculable speed, striking for his unprotected face — a part of the human anatomy by far most vulnerable and least easily treated for snake bite.

As still as death he crouched, while the still noon air was filled all about him by that vibrant rattle. Gray Dawn, pressing close behind him, perforce came to a halt. The narrow way was obstructed by his master's immobile body.

The crushed-cucumber stench of the snake, sickeningly noticeable now to the man, was tenfold so to the collie. The dog read the scent as clearly as he read the whirr. Alert, he stood, seeking the danger. For, though dogs fear poison serpents as they fear almost nothing else, the great collie did not flinch. He seemed to know his master's dire peril and to long to be of help.

Perhaps it was only a minute or two that Guy Manell crouched there, though he could have sworn it was a century. Through the whizz of the rattles, he could hear his own heart's hammering. It seemed to shake his body, the body he sought to make statue-quiet. He caught himself wondering if the throb of his blood could possibly be making his frame pulsate; and if the serpent could detect the motion and would take it as hostile. There he crouched, trying not to breathe.

Above blazed the incredibly blue California sky, with speck-like buzzards drifting through its upper spaces on flattened serrated wings. Around piled the gray peaks, barren and gaunt. Everywhere loomed the awful silent peace of the mountains — everywhere except in this single long notch of weed-grown rock where a man crouched awaiting one of death's most cruel forms.

Then, after ages of moveless tension, Guy's straining ear could catch a faint slither and rustle in the patch of whitened dry grass. He drew air into his bursting lungs in one cautiously long inhalation. For he knew he had won the waiting game. Unless some complication should intervene, he was safe.

Come suddenly upon a rattlesnake; and it will drop its inborn timidity in order to defend itself, if there be no time nor space for escape. Give it half a chance to get away — except possibly in the skin-shedding season when it is purblind and angrily terrified at everything — and it will avail itself of the chance.

Thus, when Manell did not attack, the snake began to retreat, waiting only long enough to assure itself that there was no danger in uncoiling.

For an uncoiled snake cannot strike with any strength or certainty; and a rattler will not uncoil while it thinks there is danger.

For another half-minute, Manell crouched there. Then, very slowly, he began to draw backward, taking care that no suddenness of action should alarm the snake afresh. The whizz of the rattling had ceased.

Gradually the man raised himself to his full height, disregarding his uncertain foothold. With his face and hands out of reach — since a rattler can strike for but a part of its own length — he felt safe. His thick brogans and puttees were sufficient armor.

As he gained his feet, the cracking of a dead branch under his heel agitated the tall grass. The whirring broke forth again, a yard or so back of its former location.

Vexed at his own recent fright and at its cause, Guy thrust Gray Dawn behind him. Then, risking a tumble in the narrow and rocky foothold, he strode forward.

Six feet in front of him, in the center of a grass tuft, was the snake, freshly coiled and with arrow-shaped little head poised. It seemed like some gruesome guardian of the path.

In two strides, Manell was upon it. Letting the savage headstroke smite harmless against the calf of one of his pigskin puttees, he drove his other heel with full force down upon the coiled back of the serpent.

The path was clear. Kicking aside the smashed

reptile, Guy made his way onward and upward, through the widening groove, the gray dog shivering at his side. In a quarter-hour more, he stood safely on the summit of the groove, where it debouched onto the rock-strewn platform of the second and higher and wider ledge of the mountain-face.

There, breathing a bit heavily, he stopped to rest, leaving his collie to stray about the platform and to sniff and explore a dozen alluring new smells that none but a canine nose could note. On two sides, the world was shut out from Guy's vision by the sky-piercing wall of the gray mountain. But, from this great height, he could see on two other sides for an unbelievable distance.

Far in front he saw the ridge-foot winding down the pass to where it met the Bakersfield road, beyond the corner of the Mohave Desert. There, a gray sword splitting the green valley, lay the wonder-road — perhaps like none other on earth — the concrete road that runs from the foothills straight into Bakersfield, something like twenty-eight miles away — the road that might well have been laid out with a twenty-eight-mile ruler. It deviates scarcely a hair's breadth, for the full distance; but lies level and unwinding between the poppy-and-lupin fields and the ranches and villages that line it.

In the other direction, Guy could see a patch of his own emerald fields and an angle of his cottage roof, among the tossing miles of hills that girt Friendly Valley. Beyond — and here his eyes reluctantly focused — was visible a tawny barren hillslope at whose lower end was the miserable tent-and-lean-to shack of the Graemes.

Crystal-clear was the air at this height. It enabled Guy to see not only the Graeme shack, but two people just seating themselves to luncheon at a rough board table in front of the tent-flap door. Far away they were. Yet through the dry atmosphere, Manell was certain he recognized them as Klyda and Saul Graeme. He felt there could be no mistaking either.

Having regained his breath Guy turned about, facing inward. He was just in time to see a shaking of leaves in a chaparral hedge, a furlong beyond, near the summit of a subsidiary peak which was almost on a level with the ledge.

The quiver was caused by the swift withdrawal of a human body from his sight. Someone, at the outer rim of the hedge, evidently had been watching Manell. As Guy turned, the man shrank back into the chaparral to avoid being seen.

Quickly as he moved, the suddenness of Guy's turning motion was a fraction of a second too quick. Thus, Manell not only saw the chaparral heave and open and close around a thickset body, but he caught a fleeting glimpse of the man's face.

Lightning-brief as was the glimpse and great as was the distance, Guy was dumbfoundedly aware that he recognized the lion-like head and heavy features of Saul Graeme.

Then, the face was gone; and the chaparral hedge was still and impenetrable to the eye.

"I'm letting that Graeme outfit get on my nerves!" Manell told himself, crossly, as he rubbed his eyes and glanced about him. "Five seconds ago I saw Saul Graeme sitting down to lunch in front of his own shack. And now I see him looking across at me, more than five miles away. If I'm getting to mistake every bindle stiff or hiker for one of the Graemes, it's time to stop thinking about them. They —"

He broke off, looking stupidly around him. He was standing at the rock-piled top of the groove. Nothing could go past him, either to or from the ledge, without his knowledge. Gray Dawn had run onto the ledge ahead of him. Yet Gray Dawn was no longer in sight upon the wide curving platform of rock.

Manell looked back at the Graeme shack. There was nobody, now, sitting at the table. No one was visible anywhere.

Guy stared blankly. A few bunches of vegetation (including one or two low clumps of chaparral that grew close to the inner angle of the rock-wall) alone broke the boulder-scattered bareness of the ledge. If the collie had ventured too close to the verge and had lost his footing —

Guy shouted his dog's name at the top of his lungs, at the same time hurrying to the brink to peer over.

But, at the first call, Gray Dawn reappeared. He emerged from a flattish clump of chaparral that spread, fanwise, across a spot where the mountain wall jutted out beyond the far end of the ledge.

The clump, though dense as ink, did not seem deep enough to harbor the dog's entire body. Guy frowned musingly. Then he crossed to the corner. The dog came trotting forward to meet him, surprised at the vehemence wherewith his master had bellowed his name.

"Back, Dawn!" ordered Guy, pointing to the clump, and smitten by a fantastic idea. "Back! In there again!"

Obediently, Gray Dawn turned and entered the copse. Close behind him hurried Manell, parting the bushes where they closed behind the dog's gray body.

The copse, slight in actual width, was cunningly devised to serve as a natural curtain. It masked an irregular hole in the rock-face, perhaps three feet high and two feet wide — a hole that no human eye could possibly have discerned, through that flat living screen of interwoven leaves and twigs. Nor would any human have thought of exploring the few thick bushes which seemed to grow against the sheer surface of the wall.

Thrilled, in spite of himself, Guy stooped and crawled in through the aperture, after the collie. If this were the entrance to a mountainside cave or a prehistoric mine-shaft, there might very well be a goodly store of water in it. Possibly there was a spring whose surface seepage accounted for the greenness of the scant vegetation along the inner wall of the ledge — even as springs were supposed to account for the verdure on Grudge Mountain's crest, far above. If so, the vexing water-problem would perhaps be solved, both for himself and for the Graemes.

Into the hole the man scrambled, on all fours. Touching the upper surface with the top of his head, as he crept along, he found it extended at the same height, for perhaps five feet. Then his upthrust head no longer touched the rock roof of the hole.

Cautiously he rose to his feet, expecting his scalp to collide with the cave top. But it did not. He lifted one arm high above his head. Even yet, he did not feel the roof.

Somewhere just in front of him, Gray Dawn growled thunderously. Then his bark set the echoes to resounding in deafening fashion from fifty directions. With a start, Guy Manell dropped his own uplifted arm. But his hand did not fall to his side. On its downward way, it struck against something. Instinctively Guy's fingers closed about the object they had touched.

He found himself grasping another hand — a mighty hand, damp and cold as ice, and fully three times the size of his own.

As though the contact were a signal, the long-drawn whir-r-r of a "side-winder" rattlesnake sounded in the blackness, almost at his feet.

Chapter 10

Manell was accounted a plucky man among plucky men. He had been decorated for reckless bravery, in France. He had been promoted for like cause. More than once in his twenty-eight years he had looked, full and without fear, into the icy face of death.

But now he did not scruple to spin about with the speed of a teetotum and to bolt for the dim flecks of light which betokened the presence of the chaparral-masked opening of the cave. He called to the fiercely barking collie, as he went.

Onto his knees he threw himself, as a rap on the head apprised him he had reached the low passageway leading out to the ledge. On hands and knees he shuffled forward at a rate that would have won him a first prize in any four-legged gymkhana race. Through the chaparral he butted his way, Gray Dawn close at his heels.

The dog obeyed his master's summons with strong reluctance; glaring back into the cavern, with bared fangs. His throat shook with hate-growls.

Out onto the brightly sunlit ledge plunged Guy, at a pace which well-nigh took him over its brink. Then, leaping up, he whirled to face the masked entrance; as though expecting the owner of the gigantic ice-cold hand to stalk forth and assail him.

But the cunningly devised curtain of leaves and boughs had settled back into place as he and the dog rushed out through it. No rustle nor motion of the thicket betokened pursuit.

Manell drew a deep breath. No longer ridden by crazy fear of the unreal, he was ready for whatsoever might befall him, out there in God's clean sunlight and with a normal world about him.

"What — what *was* he?" Guy babbled to himself in stark wonder. "If the rest of him was as large in proportion as his hand, he must have been fifteen feet tall and built like Goliath. He — yes, he must have been as tall as that. For his hand was sloping downward; and my own hand was about at a level with my head. And — and then that rattler close beside him on the floor! Dawn, what were *you* after, so savagely, in there? You wouldn't bark and snarl that murderous way at a rattler. How about it, Dawn? Lord, if only you could talk!"

Bit by bit Guy fell to analyzing the queer situation.

There, in that angle of ledge and wall was an opening — an opening obviously masked by human ingenuity in the training and draping of the chaparral fan and in the augmenting of its natural foliage's thickness. Within was a cavern, higher in roof than he could reach. In that cavern was a silently terrible guardian of the place, a giant whose ice-cold hand was thrice the size of a normal man's. There, as an auxiliary guard, was a "side-winder" rattlesnake!

The whole thing was nonsensical — beyond all bounds of reason. Yet — Guy had experienced it.

He knew well that there is no human being, now extant on earth, fifteen feet tall and with a hand as huge and as horrific to touch as the hand which, for the merest fraction of a second, he had found himself grasping. Yet, he *had* gripped that giant hand, clammy and ice-chilled and terrifying. He had not been dreaming nor delirious.

He had touched that hand! In imagination, he still could feel its awful contact.

As to the rattlesnake, cooler thoughts told him there might be nothing unusual about the reptile's presence there. Grudge Mountain, like several other peaks in the Sierras, was infested by these reptiles — fat, short, obscene, deadly. He had encountered such a one on his climb of the grove.

This ledge might well be the sunning-place for many rattlers. What more natural than that some of them should make their lair in the cavern behind the chaparral screen? He or Gray Dawn had chanced to tread near where one of them was slumbering. The serpent had awakened, and had rattled at them in warning. That was all.

But the hand — the impossible giant hand — ?

"There's no sense going back there, now, to explore," Manell confided to the angry dog. "I've been through my pockets. Not a match in any of them. And I'm coward enough to be mighty glad. Because if I had matches — well, for my own self-respect, I'd have to go back and investigate."

Dawn, for once, paid no heed to his loved master's mumblings. The collie was still eyeing the masked entrance. His teeth were bared. His hackles were bristling. He had shifted his shimmering gray body between Manell and the opening, as though to guard the man from some unseen mortal danger.

Guy noted his collie's behavior. It added to his own dull perplexity. He continued his half-coherent musings:

"But only a suicidal fool would crawl back, without a light, into a cave that's festooned with cranky rattlers, Gray Dawn. To say nothing of the Hand and the giant behind it. Dawn, it felt as if he was groping for me in the dark there. If I hadn't let go and jumped back as quick as I did, he'd have grappled me. What chance would any mortal have had against him, there in his own cave? No, Dawn, we didn't get out any too soon! Come on home."

Like thousands of other lonely humans, the man long since had fallen into a habit of talking to his dog. As a rule, Gray Dawn was vastly flattered thereby. But now even the several repetitions of his own name, in the course of the rambling monologue, could not turn his grim attention from the cavern mouth. Sullenly he followed his master, looking back snarlingly at intervals.

Even as he made his way back toward the groove, Guy Manell knew that for his own manhood's sake, he must come here anew as soon as he could equip himself for the exploit. He must investigate the mystery that had made him run.

"We'll go home, Dawn," he went on, as they started down the groove. "We'll go home and get a couple of strong flashlights and extra batteries and my .45, and a mouthful of lunch. Then, we'll hot-foot back here again and clear up that Jack-the-Giant-Killer puzzle. It couldn't really happen. But, Dawn, it *did* happen! I'm not going to sleep tonight, remembering how I streaked out of there — unless I can remember, too, that I went back later, like a white man, and made good. Come along. Let's hustle!"

Down the groove he made his way, far less carefully than when he had ascended it. At every moment his nerve was steadying, more and more. Instead of looking forward to the perilous and mysterious exploration as a duty to his self-respect, the spirit of adventure was beginning to stir within him. It was goading him to eager zest for the return.

High boots or puttees, and flashlight, coupled with reasonable caution, would make him immune to any or all the cave's rattlesnake tenants. As for the giant — Guy feared no foe he could see. If the man were of human size, there would be no need for weapons. If he were not or if there were more of him than one — the .45-calibre army pistol would serve to protect its handler.

"How in blue blazes does he get in and out of the cave?" puzzled Manell, as he gained solid earth at the mountain-foot. "If the rest of him is as big in proportion as that hand of his, he never can get through the hole. There must be some other way. But I'm blest if I can figure what it is. Gray Dawn, I read once about a chap that went gunning for a rabbit and found a lion. You and I went on a water-hunt. And we found — what *did* we find?"

Back toward Friendly Valley and the peace of the little white ranch house, man and dog made their way. Dawn had recovered his gay spirits. He had put from his mind the incident of the cavern and the nameless thing that had roused his jolly soul into fury. Which is the philosophical habit of the normal outdoor dog. Nor did it mean that Dawn had forgotten or would forget what had happened. Merely that there was no sense in brooding over it at a moment when such brooding could serve no sane purpose. Time enough to tackle the problem again when his master should not be there to call him away from the adventure.

Meanwhile, the world in front of him was sunlit and green and monstrous attractive. There were ground-squirrels to scent out and to chase, during the homeward trip. There were numberless alluring smells and sights to explore. Best of all, in the ranch house kitchen a goodly dinner in a goodly tin dish would be awaiting him; and there would be pints of cold water for his thirsty tongue to lap. Grudge Mountain could wait. There were more opportune things to think of just now.

This was sound philosophy, wholly canine, and beyond the scope of most humans.

Manell failed to share his collie's gift for putting futile problems behind him and for living wholly in the present. As he plodded homeward, his forehead was creased and his eyes were puckered in vain concentration. He was going over and over every detail of his morning's experiences. From every angle, possible or impossible, his thoughts were ever drawn back to the grasping of the impossible giant hand. The touch still sent shivers down his spine, at each sudden recollection of it.

He was so deep-buried in the avalanche of vain conjectures that he did not realize how near he had come to the ranch house, until Dawn wheeled aside from a squirrel chase and sprang forward with a wild-beast snarl.

Guy came out of his mooning and looked forward. The dog was rushing, head down, toward the house's front porch. There was punitive wrath in every line of his flying body. Instinctively, Guy called him back, lest the object of his raging charge might be some visiting ranch-neighbor. Sullenly the dog came to heel, still growling.

On the edge of the porch sat a man in black. A black wideawake hat's brim cast his face into shadow. A few steps farther on, Manell saw why this shadow gave so dark a hue to the face beneath it. The visitor was a Shoshone Indian. Full-blooded, at that; no half-breed as were so many of the scattered Shoshones of the region.

Yet his clothes were well-cut and well-fitting. Nothing about his apparel suggested his race, except only the wideawake which is an integral part of almost every Indian's "dress-up" costume, no matter how the rest of him may be clad.

His shapely right hand was stroking in idle friendliness the Reverend Wilberforce's back. The raccoon was cuddled close beside the Shoshone, on the porch. As a rule he kept strangers at a distance. As a rule, too, Indians do not caress animals. Guy wondered at the unwonted happening.

He understood, too, why there had been such hate in Dawn's growl. The collie loathed the sight or scent of an Indian. More than once he had attacked such few of the Shoshones or Luiseno-Kawias as he and Guy chanced to meet during their mountain rambles. It was instinctive, in the otherwise gentle dog, this bitter aversion to Indians. Nor did there seem to be logical reason for it, unless on the grounds of a disliked alien odor.

Guy was surprised, too, that this Indian should rise and move forward to greet him. It is immemorial native custom to remain seated stolidly, in contempt or in ignorance of white-man amenities of life.

"How?" said Manell, curtly, as he looked

about for such bundle of grass baskets or of pottery or other wares as itinerant Indians hawk through the Southwest.

The Shoshone lifted his hat, in response, showing a short-cropped head of hair as black and as coarse as a bay draught-horse's tail.

"How?" repeated Guy, instinctively grunting out the words, after the approved idiotic fashion of whites who seek to converse with Indians. "You wantum speak me, huh? Come to speak to pale-face? What want? Speak um plenty quick. I in hurry."

"This is Mr. Manell, isn't it?" said the Indian, in perfect English and with quiet ease of manner. "If you are in a hurry, my business with you can wait. Perhaps you'll let me call when you have a few minutes to spare?"

He made as if to go. Manell eyed him in dull amaze. The Indian's voice and manner were those of an educated man. Yet, a single glance at him could not fail to reveal that he was a full-blooded aborigine.

"Wait," interposed Guy, detaining him, and inquisitive as to the phenomenon of such a man speaking in such a way. "What can I do for you? Be quiet, Gray Dawn!" he broke off, addressing the angry collie. "Lie down!"

"Collies don't care for people of my race, as a rule," said the Indian. "I have noticed that. And I am sorry. The loss is ours. He is a splendid specimen, if you will let me say so — even though he looks as if he would like to devour me. I have

96

seldom seen a truer type, at a bench show."

Then, as if realizing he had not answered Guy's question, the visitor went on:

"You were kind enough to ask what you can do for me. This morning I fell into talk with a man who said his name was Jenner. I met him on the Santa Dereta road. He said he had been working here, and that he was leaving. He said you are short-handed."

"I am. But I —"

"I have no references with me. But if you will give me his job, I believe I can do the work satisfactorily. I had a little experience, during vacation-time, years ago, working for vine-growers up in the San Joaquin."

Guy stared doubtfully at him. Though a scatter of Indians hired out to work on California ranches, they were not in the least the type of this man.

Chapter 11

"You talk as if a desk job was more in your line than unskilled labor," said Guy. "And anyhow, you ought to have looked up my foreman, instead of me."

"I believe in going directly to the top, when I want anything," was the calm answer. "If your foreman had been prejudiced because I had no references as a vineyard-worker or because I am a Shoshone and not a white man, he would have turned me off. Then, for the sake of ranch discipline, you could not have hired me. Whereas, if you decide to hire me, your foreman will have to take me on, whether he wants to or not."

"I see. Good reasoning."

"As for my seeming more like a desk-worker than a roustabout, that is not my fault. When I left Carlisle, I planned to be a desk-worker. Perhaps, in time, something much greater. But who will hire an Indian as a clerk or a bookkeeper? Or, having hired him, who will promote him, as long as there is a white man to be promoted? So I had to drift back to this sort of thing, to keep me alive."

Amusedly, Manell listened. The man was a new specimen to him — a talkative and highly educated Shoshone. Moreover, Guy stood in sore need of an extra worker or two, especially now that Jenner had left him. This applicant was slenderly strong of build; and he claimed to have some experience in vineyards. Aloud, Guy said, hesitantly:

"It's too bad you have no references. If you had —"

"You hire bindle stiffs, you ranchers," answered the Indian. "In fact, Jenner seems to be one of them. How many of them have references?"

"H'm!" muttered Guy, this view of the case striking him for the first time.

"They are white men," pursued the Shoshone. "So, though many of them are jailbirds and many more of them ought to be, you take them on, without a line of reference. Often they are not even from an agency. As a matter of fact, isn't it in my favor that I have no references? I could have written glowing recommendations and signed them with made-up names of vine-growers somewhere on the far side of the mountains. That is often done. You would have been none the wiser."

Guy laughed. Taking out his slip-pad and pencil, he began to scribble.

"Give this to my foreman, over at the south vineyard — or else at the vineyard across that knoll," said he. "You'll find him in one of those places. If you don't find him somewhere else. I'm telling him to give you a job at $3.25 as a start and then to boost you to $3.50 if you make good.

He'll find out, in short order, whether or not you're what we want. By the way, what's your name?"

"Smith is as good a name as any," suggested the Shoshone, bitterness underlying his deep voice. "It doesn't matter what name I give. The foreman and the gang will call me 'Injun,' anyhow."

"I asked your name," Guy reminded him, sharply.

"My name," replied the Shoshone, in instant change of manner, "is Tawakwina. It signifies 'Stony Mountain.' It is a chief's name, by rights," he added, with a tinge of sadness. "But what is a chief without a people?"

"When I was a kid," said Manell, touched, despite himself, at the tone and words, "I had to learn 'Logan's Speech.' Where he tells his woes and the woes of Indians in general. I didn't know real-life Indians felt that way."

"I don't know that they do," replied Tawakwina, his manner once more aloofly noncommittal. "And if they do, it profits them nothing. ('Logan's Speech' was a fraud, you remember — written by a white man.) There is no folly so idle as to weep for what can never be regained. My fathers invaded this western land. They drove out an older and weaker race. Just as that race had driven out a still older and weaker race in the ancient days."

"So I've read."

"Then came the white man and seized the

land from my fathers — the land my fathers had seized. That is the law of nature. Even as it will be nature's law when a race of superior humans shall descend upon this land and take it from the whites. There is no cause for tears or for laments. Or for *tcikoitoa* — for grudge."

"Grudge," echoed Guy, unconscious that he had spoken, as he glanced up at the frowning gray mountain.

The Indian had not heard or else did not heed the interruption. In the same impersonal tone he continued:

"My father died when I was a child. My uncle made the error of sending me to school and then to Carlisle, to educate me for my own betterment and for the betterment of my people. He did not know I should become merely an educated savage. He was a chief — though only the chief of one or two ragged and homeless people. I am a chief in rank — but of no people at all. . . . Thank you for the job. I shall try to make good. Also it will be pleasant to eat three meals a day, once more."

Taking the slip of paper, he set off in quest of the foreman. Guy, impatient at the delay, went to the front porch and called to Sing to bring lunch to him.

"What Injun-boy want?" the Chinaman ventured to inquire as he set the meal on the porch table.

"A job," replied Guy, absently. "I gave him one."

"Umph!" sniffed Sing, in an audible aside. "Too bad! Vel' too bad! Hard 'nough for us Mel'c'ns to get job, 'thout give job to foreigner like Injun-boy!"

Disgruntled, he shuffled off to his kitchen, to brood on the criminal folly of giving work to outlanders while so many of his fellow-Americans stood in need of it. Manell ate hurriedly, his mind already running ahead to the Grudge Mountain adventure he was planning for the afternoon.

However, he was destined to longer delay than he had expected. For as he was finishing the bolted repast, a visitor, incredibly ancient and shrunken, came chugging up to the gate in a disreputable old runabout — a visitor whom Guy could not well refuse to see and whom he could not even send about his business.

Old Man Negley was the county's foremost grape-broker. He was an able and shrewd business man, despite his ninety-one years. On his cooperation depended much of Manell's success. Guy owed many favors to the eccentric old fellow. Thus he postponed the Grudge Mountain exploration whereto he had keyed himself, until his guest should see fit to move on.

"Hello, Guy!" greeted Negley, getting rheumatically out of his car and stumping toward the veranda. "I just got a hot tip. Or a chilly tip. From the Department of Agriculture. There's liable to be a twenty per cent slump in the California grape market, this year. Thought I'd stop by and tell you. Nothing like cheering a friend along, you know."

Manell's heart sank. The "twenty per cent slump," of which the old broker spoke so gaily, was due to tear wide holes in his own none-too-great profits.

"You're the fifth grower I've told that to, this day," continued Negley. "All of you look at me as if I was an accident on my way to happen. It's fine to be so popular."

"I only know one man as likely to be so popular," rejoined Guy, "and that's the inventor of the San José scale. Or the man who invented taxes. Do you expect an ovation and a cheerleader when you come around with such filthy news?"

"Son," grinned the old man, "I don't believe there's anyone in the state who has lived to see so many ups and downs in the California grape industry as I have. I've always been in it, one way or another. Ever since I drifted hereabout on my way to the gold-fields. As a half-baked kid, with my dad. That was in 1851. The year Haraszthy started the whole business. The year he made his first experiments. Growing muscatels from the seeds he picked out of imported raisins."

"Haraszthy? He —"

"I've seen you grape-men happy. And I've seen you unhappy. I've seen it so often it don't matter to me. Not any more. I saw raisin-growers getting rich quick. Back in 1890. When they got five cents a pound for raw crops. Then I saw the same men threatening to blow holes in the brains they didn't possess. When the same grade of raisins tumbled to three-quarters of a cent a pound, in 1897. I saw the wine-grape outfits bellering their hearts out and preparing to put up the shutters. That was in 1919. When they figured they'd never again get $15 a ton. On account of Prohibition. I saw the same outfits eating radium sandwiches. That was two years later. When their crop sold on the New York auction docks at ten times as much."

"But —"

"Oh, I've seen it all, sonny! So you can't expect me to shed a bucket of tears. Not when," drawing a long envelope from his pocket and running his eye down its single sheet of governmental paper, "when Husmann writes me this. From the Bureau of Plant Industry: 'From present reports it would seem that prices for your grapes this year will be 20% lower than last year.' "

He seated himself in the most comfortable chair on the porch and lighted an elderly and ill-smelling pipe. A phrase in his harangue stuck in Guy's mind, because of the odd train of thought he himself had been following for the past hour.

"You say you've been knocking around this locality, off and on, since 1851," he began. "Did you ever happen to hear of — ?"

"Yep," assented the garrulous ancient. "I blew into Kern County, first, in June 1851. As a knee-high brat. With my dad. Like I just said. Pizen hot it was, that month. And pizen lonesome, those days. In any month at all. Mainly Greasers and Injuns. Only a half-handful of white pioneers. Pioneers who were getting wise that California's wealth was in its crops. Not in its gold. If I'd had the sense then that I've got now, I'd be living in a palace somewhere. Instead of brokering grapes. For a lot of cusses that want to kick me every time I bring 'em a peckle of bad news. I —"

"Did you ever happen, in the old days," insisted Guy, raising his voice to stem the current of garrulity, "to hear rumors of — of any strange race of men or — well, or giants — that inhabited these mountains? I suppose there are always rumors or fairy tales or —"

"Rumors and fairy tales," chuckled Old Man Negley. "Yep. A plenty of 'em. Everywheres. In a new country. Like this one was, then. It was one of those fairy tales that brought me and a passel of other suckers skyhooting south here again. From Calaveras, in 1870. Things were petering out, up there. And along comes an Injun. With a yarn about oodles and roodles of gold. Piled up somewhere in these mountains. By some extinct white race. Yep, it sounds silly enough, now. But in those days the wilder a gold yarn was, the likelier it was to be true. Down I came. Along with a lot of others. Some of 'em hunted long, for the gold. And some of 'em hunted short. But all of 'em had the same brand of luck. No luck at all. I was one of the first to stop being a gold-fool and try my hand at ranching. The rest —"

His senile jaw drooped, in blank astonishment. He was staring over Manell's shoulder. Guy, from his seat on the top of the steps, turned to see what had so stricken the old man.

Chapter 12

Across the meadow from the bridge were advancing Saul and Klyda Graeme. They were walking fast, their footsteps silent on the soft grass. Almost they had reached the foot of the steps, before Old Man Negley and Guy saw them. Klyda was pale. Her face wore a troubled aspect, as of haunting fear. Her father was grimly disturbed in look and manner.

Before either of them could speak, Old Man Negley had heaved himself painfully from his easy chair and was lumbering across the porch toward them.

"Merciful snakes!" he shrilled, in noisy excitement. "If it isn't Saul Graeme! Why, man, I — I've not clapped eyes onto you, this fifty years or more! Yep, *more'n* fifty years. You haven't changed. Not a mite. Except you're some better dressed. And a whole lot cleaner than when you and me shared the same blanket. And the same dinged coffee pot!"

He had grasped both the hands of Saul Graeme and was wringing them with all his aged strength, in an access of tumultuous welcome.

Guy and Klyda looked from one man to the other in frank bewilderment. Manell knew Saul Graeme could not possibly be more than fifty

107

years old, at most. Yet here was this mummy-like antique hailing him familiarly and affectionately by name, and assuring him that he had not "changed a mite" in more than a half-century. The thing was absurd!

From the delighted Negley, the onlookers' glances focused on Graeme, to see how he would take this incredible greeting.

For an instant, Saul's lined face was as blank as Klyda's own. Then he flushed. His astonished eyes fell. He seemed embarrassed, even profoundly uncomfortable. To Guy's quickened imagination he had the air of a man whose closest-guarded secret is in danger of detection.

"Why!" cried Klyda, breaking the moment of dumbfounded silence. "My father was a baby, fifty years ago, sir! You're thinking of someone else."

"A baby, hey?" challenged Old Man Negley. "He was older'n I was. He must have been a good seven or eight years older. I was the 'baby'! Not him. If I hadn't been, would I have let him fool me into another wildgoose gold-hunt through these stepladder mountains? After I'd settled down, all sane and snug, on my own good ranch? After I'd put all that gold-silliness behind me? We had a mighty interesting summer. So far as fun went. Saul and I did. He's good company. I'll grant him that. And he has got a way with him. But we never got a pinch of gold. Not big enough to choke a flea. He was —"

The cloudy old eyes puckered into sudden disturbing thought. Again the tremulous jaw drooped. The brief excitement faded from Negley's face, leaving it pitifully empty, like a confused small boy's. He blinked at the embarrassed Saul. Then he mumbled:

"I — I — That is — You'll have to excuse me, friend. I'm an old man. Horribly old. My mind don't run one hundred per cent true. Like it once did. I was kind of carried out of myself. Just for the minute. I'm asking your pardon. It's the first time my brain ever went clean off the trolley. The way old folks' brains are supposed to do, sometimes."

He looked perplexedly into Saul's embarrassed face. Then he added, in explanation:

"I was ninety-one, last week, stranger. And you can't be much more'n half that. I see now I've been talking to you like a fool. When I said I knew you, more'n fifty years ago. I — Manell, I guess I'll trot on, now. It's a hot day. I'll just chug home. Home. And lie down for a spell."

Awkwardly, much ashamed of himself for his aged mind's blunder, he hobbled at top speed toward his car, not once looking back.

"A little crazy, I suppose?" ventured Saul, as Negley departed.

"He has the name for being one of the shrewdest business men in this part of California," answered Guy. "I can't understand how he could have —"

"And Dad," put in Klyda, mystified, "he called you by your own name. That was the funny part of —"

109

Abruptly she fell silent, at a swift look of rebuke from her father. Graeme turned to his host with evident eagerness to change the subject.

"Mr. Manell," said he, "you will pardon our intruding on you again in this way. If only ourselves were involved, we would not have done it. But this seems to concern you, as well."

As he spoke, he handed Guy a folded sheet of paper he was carrying. It was of the same kind as those whereon the two warnings had been written — coarse brownish paper, twenty by twenty inches.

"This was lying on my father's bed," explained Klyda, speaking coldly, yet with a tremor of anxiety in her clear voice, "when we came into the shack from lunch, less than an hour ago. It must have been left there by someone who crept in by the back way, while we were eating at the outdoors table in front. My father wanted to come here alone with it. But I —" the clear voice breaking ever so little, "I don't want him out of my sight, if he is really in danger."

Guy was unfolding the crackling paper and studying its scrawled message. In the same thick reddish fluid as before were scribbled the painstakingly illiterate words:

"*Yuve had one warrning. So has Mannel. Dont wate for the next one eether of yu as it wont be safe for yu to wate. Go wile yu can go alive.*"

"You have had a warning like this?" asked Graeme, his face no longer concealing his real worry.

"Yes," said Guy. "A little while after you left here, yesterday afternoon. But this is the second you've had, today. Our anonymous friend seems even more interested in you than in me. Unless," he added, "unless —"

Then he stopped short, his suspicion of the Graemes stirring to fresh life. There seemed no sense in these elaborately ill-spelt melodramatic threats. He saw no reason why he and the Graemes should be coupled in them.

His own warning had come just after he had met them. Now they claimed to have had two such messages in a single day. If for any cause the Graemes were interested in getting him out of the region — though the thought seemed absurd — they were going about it in a most systematic, mysterious way. There seemed no other solution.

"Unless?" prompted Klyda, as he paused.

"Nothing," he made curt reply.

She looked at him in unhappy wonder.

"And," he pursued, jarred by the look, "if you chance to meet the person who is doing this, will you kindly tell him he is wasting cheap paper and cheaper hand-made illiteracy in trying to scare me? I am here. I have been here, three years. Here I am going to stay. This is the twentieth century, not the fifteenth. With the coming of the movies, the last bit of tinsel real-life melodrama went out of fashion."

"But," she persisted, though visibly hurt by his manner, "why should the warning come to *both* of us? To you as well as to us? Why should the same person want us out of the way that wants you out of the way? What connection?"

"None that I can see," he returned icily, angry at himself that the girl's presence should make it so hard for him to maintain his resentment toward her. "Coincidence, perhaps. Coincidences are queer things, you know. For instance, in 1840, William Henry Harrison was elected President of the United States. He died in office. Twenty years later, Abraham Lincoln was elected President. He died in office."

"What has that to do with — ?"

"Twenty years later, Garfield was elected President. He died in office. Twenty years later, McKinley was elected, to his second term as President. He died in office. Twenty years later, Harding was elected President. He died in office. In other words, every twenty years, for nearly a century — 1840, 1860, 1880, 1900, 1920 — a president has been elected who was fated to die in office. Watch for the man who'll be elected President in 1940. I wouldn't want his job, if there's anything in the twenty-year death sequence. All coincidence, of course, but a bit strange, at that. Well, if the twenty-year series is a coincidence, this coupling of you people with me, in the warning, may be a coincidence, too. There can be no sane reason for it. Or can there?"

He had spoken ramblingly and with irrelevant wordiness, to regain control of himself and to fight back the odd sensation of having spoken harshly to a clean-souled child.

The girl continued to look at him for an instant, with that glint of pain and bewilderment in her big eyes. Then, wearily, she said to her father:

"Shall we go?"

For the second time that day, Guy made no effort to check their departure. Mutely he watched them as they made their way back across the meadow to the bridge and the road which led to their forlorn dwelling.

"If they were on the square," he murmured to himself, "this would be a dirty way for me to treat two homesick folk from my own part of the world. I wish to the Lord they *were* square. At least, I wish that *she* was. How did Providence ever happen to put eyes like those in the face of a girl who can lie the way she does? . . . I'm a fool to keep on thinking about her!"

To distract his thoughts he made ready for the postponed return journey to Grudge Mountain. Going indoors, he got his service pistol and strapped it to his belt. Then he pocketed two flashlights and, as a precaution, took along a spare battery. Picking up his heaviest walking stick, he set forth on his adventure, calling the delighted collie to heel as he went.

While he hurried along, his mind drifted to Old Man Negley's queer hallucination about Saul Graeme. He recalled Klyda's wonder and his own, that the oldster should know her father's name; and that Negley should call him by it in mistaking him for an absent chum. Graeme's quick look of admonition as she had spoken of this incredible circumstance came back vividly to Manell, increasing the muddle into which all the past day's events had thrown his ideas.

"There's a lot you and I don't understand, Dawn," he confided to the flatteringly attentive collie. "And the little we do understand, we don't like. Why do a lot of miserable puzzles and mysteries have to come butting into our life here, after we've gotten on so comfy, all these years? Why does *she* have to — ?"

His muttered train of thought was shattered.

He had been striding along at mile-eating speed, through the foothills. Now, passing the spot where he had met Klyda, he rounded the bend and came in full view of the lower slope of Grudge Mountain. There, in front of him, in the dazzle of an afternoon light, rose the precipitate rock walls, with their balcony-like upper and lower ledges. There, too, was the groove, leading up to the end of the higher ledge.

But the mass of rocks, which had been banked at the ledge's extreme end, to the far side of the groove and just over it, were gone, leaving a clear space of ledge and of wall directly above. They had not vanished into air, these cluttered tumuli of prehistoric rock. They were still visible. But they had shifted their location in a wholly inexplicable way.

They had tumbled headlong into the long trough of the groove. Now, they blocked the narrow center of the trough and all the space above that thin passage. From halfway up, almost to the surface of the ledge itself, the groove was choked by scores of immense boulders, some of them many tons in weight.

No human — no mountain goat — could have passed through or over that high-piled barrier of stones, which bulged far to either side of the groove, cutting off all possible means of ascent.

"Lucky the landslide didn't come while I was up there!" thought Manell. "I'd have been stranded on the ledge till eternity."

Then as his practiced eye studied the choked groove, he exclaimed aloud:

"Good Lord! That was no landslide. A lot of those biggest rocks were too far to one side for them to have been caught and sent down; even if the pile from above had gotten loosened. There's not a loose rock left on the whole ledge!"

He stared up, agape.

"Dawn!" he said, a tinge of awe in his whispered voice. "It would have taken twenty skilled men a week or more to pry all those biggest boulders off the ledge and steer them down the groove. It — it couldn't have been done in the two or three hours since you and I were here. It couldn't! But — but it *was!* Grudge Mountain's secret is corked up forever, now."

He ceased his slurred mutterings. In sudden anger he shook his fist up at the ledge.

"Whoever you are, up there," he yelled in a defiance as fierce as it was foolish, "I'm going to get you, soon or late! You're not going to scare me again with your silly bugaboo stunts. I'm no baby. *I'm going to get you!* It's a finish fight, from now on!"

He checked his yelled challenge, realizing suddenly his mental and emotional likeness to a puppy that bays the moon.

Chapter 13

The solid fact remained that, within the space of a quarter-day, tons of rock had been removed from their places along the surface of the ledge and from the pile that had stood for ages beside the top of the groove. They had been tossed with mathematical precision into the trough, in such a way as to block any possible chance of ascending its steep course.

Manell climbed up, as far as he could struggle, only to be brought to a standstill by the impassable rock-barrier which towered high above his head. He sought to scale this, by swarming up to the top of the nearest giant boulder which obstructed his path.

His weight caused the ill-balanced rock to topple. He sprang back into the groove and threw himself on his face there, among the undergrowth, just in time to avoid the displaced boulder as it rumbled downward above him, held to its course for a space by the upjutting sides of the groove. Then, from its own momentum, it bounced clear of the impeding groove-walls and sprang out into space, crashing noisily to the rubble-strewn base of the wall.

Shivering at his bare escape, Guy forbore to court death by further effort to scale the uncertain rock-jam which filled the groove. He made his way to the ground below, and stared again at the baffling heights. Directly above him, hundreds of feet up, jutted the ledge. So far as his reaching it was concerned, it might as well have been in the planet Neptune.

There, at its farthest corner from the groove, he knew, was the fan-shaped clump of chaparral which masked the cunningly hidden entrance to the cavern — the cavern wherein his groping fingers had closed upon that icily dread giant hand! But the mystery seemed in a fair way to remain unsolved until Doomsday, despite his wild brag that he would find some means of clearing it.

Around the mountain-base Guy retraced his steps. He passed beyond the point where the great upper ledge merged with the almost perpendicular surface of the cliff. A few rods farther on, began the outjut of the smaller and lower ledge, far beneath the higher one, and less broad.

Walking back until he could study the verge of this, Guy inspected it. Yes, it was much lower than the great ledge which he could no longer hope to reach. An active man with catlike qualities of climbing and with a clear head and good wind might possibly succeed in squirming his way up to it at one end, where the less clifflike slope of mountain and the various faults in the rock and one or two clinging dwarf pines gave promise of foot-and-hand hold of a precarious sort.

At that one corner only was there a bare

chance of scaling to the lower ledge. Even a professional climber would run at least a seventy-five per cent risk of a broken neck in the attempt. Yet, as Guy could see from below, there seemed nothing to be gained by ascending to this lesser ledge. It was not only far beneath the upper one and the mysterious cavern, but it was almost equally far to the south of it; and with no means of communication between the two.

If he should succeed in gaining the lower ledge, he would be as far as ever from reaching the upper. There was no sense in hazarding death for such a futile achievement. As wisely climb the Woolworth Tower in an attempt to get to the stars.

Thence, as far as either ledge extended, in both directions, Manell continued his fruitless search of the mountain-base, stopping always at the foot of the choked groove to gaze in unceasing wonder at the miracle wrought there.

The more he scanned the wreckage the more calmly certain he became that it could not possibly have been caused by landslide or avalanche. Rocks that he recalled seeing on the upper ledge, far beyond the path of any such slide, were now gone from their moss-bound sockets and were amid the mass of boulders that filled the upper section of the groove.

No, it was the work of hands. That was beyond doubt. But innumerable human hands, aided by the most perfect hoisting apparatus, must needs have labored for days to achieve this Herculean task. And the work had been completed in three hours, at most.

Afternoon reddened into sunset and sunset was swept into the swift twilight of southern California. Dusk had in turn given place to darkness before Manell abandoned his utterly fruitless inspection of the place.

Then, tired and baffled, he turned home. Yet, for all his weariness, there burned ever stronger within him that strange new stubborn resolve to fight back at the mysterious forces which had blocked his way; and to wrest from them their impossible mystery.

Guy Manell was an easygoing chap, seldom troubling himself to turn out of his routine path. Such men, once roused to any difficult or out-of-the-way exploit, are tenfold harder to turn aside from it than is the normal adventure seeker.

The bulldog, despite his sinister repute, is one of the gentlest and most easygoing of animals. But once rouse him to action, and he hangs on until he is dead. It was not for nothing that Manell's good-natured face was equipped with a most serviceable bulldog jaw. Animal traits are far oftener duplicated in us humans — or perhaps human traits are far oftener duplicated in animals — than psychologists realize.

Having once set his teeth, figuratively, into this problem, Guy Manell would not let go of it until it was solved or he himself was dead. He knew that. And he wondered at the strange obsession that had seized him — the resolve that had twisted his mind from its placid course and was goading it along these tortuous new byways of mad adventure.

The miracle of the choked groove — the carefully illiterate warnings — the golden bullet that so narrowly had missed killing him and then had vanished — Jenner's unexplained fright — the Graeme puzzle — all these had stirred him to feverish and illogical anger; and they had scourged him into a flaring resolve to conquer and smash the unseen forces which seemed hemming him in.

Through the red mist of his turmoil danced ever the dainty face and the big eyes of the girl he wanted to despise and could not. This only added fuel to his wrath and force to his resolve.

To no man is it given to enjoy more than a limited period of bovine placidity. Guy Manell's pleasant era of this commodity had come, for the time, to an abrupt end.

At seven next morning Guy took the road to the Graeme ranch. He had not slept. But out of his sleeplessness had come sanity which put to flight the unwonted morbidness that had possessed him.

Forcing himself to logical reasoning, he felt he had been making a sulky idiot of himself. A girl had hurt his vanity by telling him she was going home to rest, and then by climbing the Grudge Mountain ledge, instead. That was all; when Manell stripped her conduct of useless externals. Surely there was nothing in that deception to make him go around with a grievance against her and against her father!

Graeme and Klyda had had a perfect right to go to the ledge or to go anywhere else they might choose to. They were in no way accountable to Guy for their actions. If those actions were to be shrouded in privacy, for any reason — well, hadn't they a right to deceive him about something that was no concern of his?

He had no proof that they were connected with the silly warnings he had received, nor that they had done more than try to keep him in the dark about something which was none of his business.

Yet, when they had come to him, scared and worried and in need of helpful advice, he had been chilly and even rude toward them — he an old-timer in a country where hospitality and kindness to helpless newcomers is a fixed rule!

He was ashamed of himself for his dearth of neighborly courtesy. Refusing to admit, even to himself, that this, his new viewpoint, was influenced by his haunting desire to see Klyda again and once more to be on the pleasant terms which had marked their first day's acquaintance, he resolved to go straight to the Graemes and to offer to be of any possible service to them, in their dilemma.

None knew better than Guy the uphill task ahead of the untrained Saul, in turning his brush-grown barren tract of land into a profitable vineyard. For, though California gives generously to those who have the brain and the endurance to wrest her agricultural wealth from her, yet there is a laborious apprenticeship before fallow land, anywhere, can be made to pay dividends.

That Graeme and his delicately reared daughter should have undertaken such a task with such poor equipment, was in itself tragic. That Manell, their nearest neighbor, should have turned a cold shoulder on them was inexcusable.

Guy strode the faster. His self-contempt mounted, as he walked.

Then, he was aware that though his thoughts had been turned inward, his eyes had been subconsciously fixed on a murky cloud which hung low in air, just beyond the hillock which cut off the Graeme shack from his view.

There it hung, lowering and waving, in the still air of early morning — this cloud that could only be smoke. At the sight, Guy muttered, half aloud:

"The poor Babes in the Wood! Burning up their litter of packing boxes and other trash! When they've lived a little longer in a place where coal sells at $17 a ton, they won't throw away fuel like that."

He breasted the rise and came in sight of the side-hill ranch below him. His fast walk changed to a breakneck run. The tent-lean-to shack and its adjacent shanty-like stable were in flames.

They were three-quarters consumed. Their

flimsy material was burning like so much dry paper. Above hung the scowling black smoke that had caught Manell's attention from the far side of the knoll.

On the hillside, midway between him and the blazing shack, lay a milch cow, her throat cut as neatly as if by a professional butcher. From the dark hue of the slowly drying pool in which rested her head, she had apparently been dead for more than an hour. Just outside the door of the burning stable sprawled a dead horse — one of Graeme's team — its throat severed as had been the cow's. Its team-mate lay half in and half out of the stable door.

Chapter 14

Back and forth from their three water-barrels Graeme and Klyda were rushing, grimed and with blistered hands, carrying pails of futile water to cast on the flames. Their fire-fighting was as unskilled as it was strenuous. No expert could have quenched that blaze, with such petty materials and against such headway. On the ground were a single trunk and a bag, saved from the conflagration.

Klyda was straining under the weight of a filled bucket too heavy for her strength, as Guy came over the thick-underbrushed crest of the hillock. She was approaching the blaze with it, so closely that the heat scorched her dainty face and almost set fire to her hair.

Saul Graeme was completing a return trip to the three barrels, fifty yards distant from the shack. In each hand he swung a pail. Under his left arm was tucked his rifle. He was running, in his haste to refill the useless buckets.

All this, Guy's first sweeping glance photographed instantaneously on his brain. Then he was crashing at full tilt through the shoulder-high undergrowth, on his way down the knoll.

The shack was in a flat space of ground, with hillsides sloping away from it on two sides. The slope opposite to Guy was more thickly brush-grown than was the hillock down whose side he was speeding.

At his second step, he heard a gunshot, that re-echoed from hill to hill. Directly in front of him, from near the top of the opposite hill-slope, a plume of white powder smoke was hanging above the chaparral. At the same instant, a scream from Klyda brought Manell's gaze back to the scene below him. He was just in time to see Saul Graeme drop pails and rifle, and pitch forward across the almost emptied water-butts.

Klyda forgot the fire and all else, in her mad haste to reach the side of her stricken father. Fast as she ran, she had barely knelt beside him and caught his head in her arms, when Guy Manell was standing over her.

Looking up dazedly, she saw the young rancher. She cried out to him to hurry for a doctor. Instead, Guy moved to the other side of her, where his stocky body was between herself and the hillside whence had come the shot. Then, kneeling, he ran his hands deftly over the unconscious man and examined his clothing.

"No bullet mark on head or arms," he reported, as he worked. "No drop of blood on the shirt and no hole in it. Nor on the trousers, either. They — Here we are!" he broke off. "He isn't killed, Miss Graeme. See? The bullet went through his heavy boot, just below the knee. He has fainted from shock. . . . Keep where you are, please!" he admonished, as she made as though to come around on the other side, to look more closely at the hole he indicated, an inch below the boot-top. "If there's to be a second shot, I don't want you in line with it."

Unheeding, she leaned far forward. Shifting his position so as to come again between her slight body and the hill-slope, Manell drew off the boot as tenderly as he could. Not a drop of blood was visible on the trouser-leg. Apart from a bit of scraped surface on the khaki cloth, there was no sign of the passage of the ball.

"I saw two cases like this, in Flanders," commented Guy, his sensitive fingers busily exploring. "It's — Yes, I thought so. The range was long. The double-leather of the boot-top spent most of the bullet's force. All it did was to break the bone, with what impetus it had left. The —"

Saul Graeme gasped. A quiver ran through his body. His eyes opened dazedly. The anguish and shock of the broken bone had not power to keep a man of his tough constitution in senselessness for more than a moment or two.

The girl bent sobbing above him. Guy Manell wasted no time in sentiment. In a second, he was swinging the three water-butts, one after the other, between the wounded man and the opposite hillside.

"There!" he declared with grim satisfaction. "To get to either of you, he'll have to shoot through those. He doesn't know how near empty they are. So he won't make the try."

Oblivious of his own possible danger, he was

standing erect, scanning the distant hill-slope. Its rank brushwood was impenetrably thick, at the point whence the shot had been fired. It ran, with almost equal density, to the top of the hill.

The marksman, with any skill at all, could readily make his way, unseen, through that cover and back to the far side of the hill, and thence, through any of three routes, to the shelter of the higher mountains.

Guy was seized with a longing to rush after him, as he had after his own assailant of two days earlier — to charge through the chaparral and, if not in time to overhaul the man, at least to try to sight him from the hill's summit.

Indeed he had taken an impulsive step, when a groan from Saul recalled him to the more urgent duties of the moment. The wounded man was lying with his head supported on the white-faced girl's knee, as she sat clasping him to her. Graeme's mind was clear; but the dents about his mouth and the beads of sweat on his smoke-grimed forehead spoke eloquently of his agony.

His rolling eye turned toward the merrily roaring flames that had burned his shack and stables to the ground. Thence his gaze wandered to his slain horses and cow. Last of all, he looked down at his own broken leg.

"It's done," said Guy, simply. "Too late to mourn over it, now. You're still alive. That's the thing to remember and to be thankful for. Don't try to move or talk. Lie still."

He glanced about him. His eye fell on the light

buckboard, in the open, at some distance from the conflagration, so far away that its shabby paint was scarce blistered by the heat.

"I'm sorry it isn't something more comfortable," he mused. "But if it was, it would probably be too heavy."

Going across to the vehicle, he came back, walking between its shafts and pulling it after him.

"The days of buckboards and even of horses, in this locality, are pretty well past," he commented, cheerfully, as he ranged alongside the sufferer. "But I'm glad you didn't realize that when you came here. It solves your transportation problem."

"What do you mean?" asked Klyda, puzzled.

"I am going to lift your father onto the seat of this," answered Guy, "and wheel him back to Friendly Valley. There we'll put him to bed, and send across to Santa Dereta for Doc Vreeland to set his leg. He's the best physician and the best surgeon in the county. Perhaps the best anywhere in the state. It will hurt, sir," he went on, addressing the silent Graeme. "It will hurt you like the very mischief, to have me lift you into the wagon. And I'm afraid the jolting will hurt you a lot, too. But I'll do it all as gently as I can. And it's the only way of getting you there. I'd go and bring back a car for you. But —"

He glanced at Klyda. Graeme nodded in approval. He understood Manell's reluctance to leave her on this scene of danger with only a crip-

129

pled man to protect her, in case the unseen marksman were still lurking in the chaparral.

"You are good," said Graeme. "I thank you. Never mind the pain. I shan't make a baby of myself or make your Samaritan task any harder for you than I can help."

"But —" began Klyda, uncertainly.

"It is the only thing to do," insisted Guy. "Your father can't be left here. My house is the nearest place where he can be comfortable. He is going there; and you are coming along to nurse him. I'll load that trunk and valise onto the back of the wagon. The one thing, now," he added, "is for us to look out for him, while he can't look out for himself. All the rest can wait. It will be time enough for him to make a new start, when he is well again. Don't let's think about it, till then."

Arranging the seat's torn corduroy cushion as comfortably as might be and placing a box in front of it to prop the broken leg on, he lifted Saul Graeme as a mother might lift her sick child.

Saul's bulk and weight threw tremendous strain on Manell's sinewy strength. But he achieved the lifting, without adding overmuch to the sick man's anguish. Laughingly he ordered aside the girl who would have shared the burden with him, bidding her guide the broken leg to its resting place on the box.

He gave mute credit to the pluck wherewith Saul endured this augmenting of his hurt. Not by sound or facial motion did the big man give sign that he was in torment. But his face was green-white.

"Be as brave as your father is," he bade Klyda, as she trembled piteously at sight of Graeme's suffering. "You have the face of a girl who could stand any amount of pain on your own account or meet any danger without collapsing. You must do as much for him as you'd do for yourself. He needs you. He will need you more when we get him home. Don't go to pieces."

He spoke gently; his voice was gentler than his words. And she responded to the needed advice by straightening and facing him calmly.

"I shan't go to pieces," said she, continuing: "You'll let me help draw the buckboard, won't you? It will be terribly hard for you to pull it up the slope."

"It'll be terribly hard for your father, bumping up the slope, unless you walk alongside to steady him," retorted Guy, taking his place in the shafts. "That's where you'll be most useful. Now, then! We're off!"

Followed a half-hour of increasingly difficult work for Manell, between the shafts, and of pain stoically borne by Saul. As the queer cortege made its slow way to Friendly Valley, Klyda told, between intervals of tending Graeme, the story of the morning's tragedy.

On the preceding afternoon, after their return from the brief visit to Guy Manell, father and daughter had talked of nothing but the two warnings. Failing to gain advice from Guy, as to what best should be done, they framed a plan of action of their own.

Graeme had pointed out the fact that both warnings must have been delivered by some mysterious person who had risked detection by bringing them thither. Such a man, he argued, was extremely likely to be watching the ranch pretty closely, from a hiding-place. Otherwise he could not have been able to choose the safe moments for leaving the messages there. Also, he would, in all likelihood, be curious to note their effect, and would thus be on the lookout.

Saul decided to give this invisible spy an answer that could not be mistaken — whether the warnings were sincere or not. Wherefore, late that afternoon, he had climbed to the top of the hillock (over whose crest Guy was now hauling him in the jouncing buckboard), carrying both the warnings with him. There, in full sight for miles around, he spread them out and held them high in air, that their nature might be visible to any onlooker. Then, still with his arms uplifted, he had torn the two big sheets of brown paper in half and had set them afire. Thereby, as he and Klyda agreed, the sender of the warnings might know how they were regarded by their recipients.

It seemed the only way to let the Unknown realize that they held his threats in contempt — that they had come thither prepared to stay and that they were not to be frightened off by cheap melodrama.

Father and daughter had sat up late that night, talking over their plans and discussing the possible effect of their burning of the sheets of paper. Thus, they overslept.

Klyda was wakened by the reek of smoke. Jumping up, she found the shack was on fire. She and Graeme had barely time to throw on their clothes and pull some of their luggage out of doors, before they saw the stables also were blazing.

During their frantic trips between the waterbarrels and the burning structures they noted the slain bodies of their livestock. Then came the shot from the hillside, and Guy Manell's providential arrival.

The bare little story left Guy marveling at the deadly and seemingly reasonless malice of the whole occurrence. Such things have been done to unpopular folk in wild neighborhoods or to families with whom a blood-feud was waged. But these Graemes were newcomers to the region. They had no foes. They had no acquaintances, except himself. Nor is southern California given to such deeds as this. It did not have rhyme nor reason to it.

For that matter, the similar warning and similar shot at himself had as little. The connection between the two sets of warnings and shots reminded him of something that had not yet occurred to him as significant. He remembered picking up Graeme's discarded boot and dropping it into the back of the buckboard.

Now, as he came to the top of the hillock and paused for a moment's breathing space, he went around to the rear of the vehicle and found the boot. Holding it upside down he shook it.

Out tumbled a glittering little object. Guy held it up to the light for the two others to see.

It was a bullet, of purest gold.

Chapter 15

Slightly flattened by its impact against Graeme's leg-bone, the golden slug nonetheless bore the unmistakable mold of a large caliber ball. There was no sign of its having borne the shape of the ordinary cartridge bullet. Apparently it had been a circular lump of gold, fashioned into a ball by some old-fashioned bullet-mold, such as had been in vogue before the day of modern cartridges.

At sight of it, Klyda Graeme's big eyes opened wider, in amaze; while her father's pain-racked features contracted.

"The same chap has been gunning for us both, Mr. Graeme," commented Guy with forced lightness, as he handed the bullet to Saul. "And with a single shot, each time. I suppose it costs too much to load up a repeating rifle with such precious ammunition. If he has anything so modern as a repeating rifle. A few more of these, and we'll be on Easy Street, you and I. We can make more money being shot at than by ranching."

Saul forced his writhen lips to a smile, in recognition of the feeble witticism. Klyda said nothing. But she pressed closer to her father.

Thus in time the buckboard came to the edge of Friendly Valley, at a spot where the foreman and every laborer were busy over the planting of a new five-acre Sultana vineyard patch. This patch was the hope of Manell's heart, against the time when the old vineyard immediately adjoining it should peter out.

Here, strong hands relieved Guy at the shafts. Hence, too, a workman was sent posthaste in Manell's car to bring Dr. Vreeland from Santa Dereta.

To inquiries, Guy said shortly that Graeme's ranch house had burned and that its owner had broken his leg while trying to fight back the flames. To have told the tale of the golden bullet would have been to give every one of his men the fixed belief that their employer was either drunk or heatstruck.

Klyda and her father, following his lead, said nothing to deny the statement. The girl followed the buckboard, at Guy's side, for the brief remaining distance to the cottage.

"I won't try to thank you for all you are doing for us, Mr. Manell," she said, as they moved on together. "I can only say I would not let you put yourself out like this, if it was not for my father's sake."

There was a hint of resentful memory in her young voice. It stung Guy to self-shame.

"Please don't talk that way!" he begged her. "I'm happier than you'd care to know, that you're both to be my guests. You don't understand how lonely I get, here, with only Sing and Gray Dawn and the Reverend Wilberforce for companionship. Besides," hesitantly, "it will make me feel less guilty for my rudeness to both of you. I've — I've been having a lot to bother and perplex me. And I'm afraid it's made me cranky — even to my two new neighbors. Will you forgive me, and let us start over again?"

He held out his hand, impulsively, as he spoke, his gaze meeting hers in boyish appeal. On impulse — all her resentment swept away — she grasped the outstretched hand in her soft little fingers. Hands and eyes met. Hands and eyes held their unconsciously eager hold for a fraction longer than civility really required. Then Klyda drew away her fingers, her tanned face flushing slightly. Guy was aware of a most astonishing throb in the region of his hitherto immune heart. The two eyed each other in swift wonder. Then Klyda's gaze dropped. Her face flushed a shade more vividly.

"Come!" she bade him, as if she were a little out of breath. "Shall we hurry? I want to be there when they lift Dad down."

"Now," wondered Manell, wordlessly, as he increased his own pace to keep up with hers, "now what in blue blazes is the idea of this? I'm — Good Lord! I hope I'm not doing anything so crazy as — Nonsense!"

He shrugged his broad shoulders impatiently, and glanced down sideways in furtive wonder, at the girl. By an odd coincidence, she chose that instant for a furtive upward glance.

Reddening, both began to speak at the same

time, to cover up the awkward moment. Then, as abruptly, both fell silent. And silent they remained until they reached the veranda to aid in lifting from the buckboard the solid weight of Saul Graeme.

The invalid was borne into the house and was ensconced in Guy Manell's own camp bed. Then, leaving him with his daughter, Guy drew aside the gloweringly indignant Sing. He bade the Chinaman prepare the adjoining office as a bedroom for Klyda. At news that there were to be guests at the ranch — one of them a woman — Sing could have wept aloud. Grumbling like a very dyspeptic old bear, he slunk off to his trebled labors.

Two hours later, Vreeland, the Santa Dereta doctor, had come and gone. He pronounced Saul's injury a simple fracture; and he prophesied that he would be walking without a crutch inside of two months. In the meantime — especially for the next few weeks — he must be kept absolutely still.

"Can't we take him to the hospital at Santa Dereta, Doctor?" asked Klyda, when she heard the verdict. "It is not fair to put Mr. Manell to all this annoyance. He —"

"Mr. Manell will let you know," put in Guy, "when it begins to annoy him."

He was absurdly happy at the physician's decree which promised to keep Klyda in the same house with him for weeks to come. At a loss to understand his own delight in the situation, he nonetheless dreaded lest the girl should deprive him of it, by taking her father to Santa Dereta. But Dr. Vreeland's next words reassured him.

"I'm sorry, Miss Graeme," said Vreeland. "But the flu epidemic has filled every private room and every ward bed at our hospital, there. It's a light form of flu, this year. Very light indeed. Not at all as it was in 1918. But people get to remembering how bad it was in that year; and they come flocking in from everywhere, to the hospital. We're putting cots in the basement and in the front yard. If Mr. Manell doesn't object to letting your father stay here, he'll be far more comfortable and he'll get much better attention than in such a crowded place. I'll look in again, tomorrow noon."

And so it was settled.

That evening, when Saul had gone into a drugged sleep, Guy and Klyda sat together on the tiny front porch. The great white California stars shone benignly down upon them from a black velvet sky; and the giant shadowy mountains stood guard above the peaceful little valley.

Guy sat there, alone, long after the girl had gone to bed. For some obscure reason the house now seemed more to him like a real home than had any dwelling-place in all his life. Musing happily on this phenomenon, he got up at last, stretching and making ready to turn in.

Gray Dawn had fallen asleep in the hallway, behind him. He did not chirp to the dog, as usual, in making his customary last round of the house and the outbuildings, before going to bed. Instead, he went alone, his moccasined feet light on the soft ground. Strolling around an angle of the nearest barn, he caught a faint glow of light behind the far corner of the wooden hay-barrack, just ahead. Curious, he stepped forward to investigate.

Guy rounded the barrack corner, just in time to see the dim bulk of a man crouching low on the ground at its far end. He was crouching beside a pile of something that had not been there that afternoon.

As Guy paused, the faint glow reappeared. The man had struck a match and was shielding it between his large palms. Apparently, the glow which had first attracted Guy's notice was from an earlier match which the wind had blown out.

The bit of light flickered low, then blazed into brief brightness. By its illumination, Manell could see the nature of the two-foot-high heap against the barrack wall and just beneath the bulging masses of stored hay. It was a pile of thin-whittled wood and shavings, intermixed with wet rags. Even at that distance, Manell got a rank whiff of gasoline from the rags.

Then, the man's arm went forward to touch his match to the gasoline-soaked stuff. As he did so a lightning-short radiance of the flame shone on his face.

The cry of fury in Guy's throat died unborn. For the sketchily and momentarily-revealed face was the face of Saul Graeme.

Chapter 16

Stupefied, Guy Manell stood at gaze. The flicker of light left the half-averted face of the incendiary. The match flare touched the inflammable pile of oil-soaked rags and shavings.

At the contact, Manell shook off the numb astonishment that had gripped him. At a bound he had reached the incipient fire. His instinct for saving his barracks and all the adjoining buildings from destruction was stronger than that for capturing the intruder. Swift as the flame sprang up, from the lighted rags, Manell was swifter. He threw himself bodily upon the newly-ignited heap, crushing out the first licking flame beneath his chest, and beating the scarce-ignited sparks with his bare hands.

It was the work of only a few seconds; for the fire had not had a fair start, nor had a single spark reached the tinder-dry hay just above. But the interval was long enough for the incendiary to leap to his feet and to break into a noiseless run which carried him so quickly out of the range of vision that he seemed rather to have melted into air than to have escaped through the gloom.

It was senseless to try to follow so wily and swift an enemy through the night. Yet as soon as he was certain the fire was out, Manell rushed in headlong pursuit.

Presently he slowed to a halt. There was no faintest sound of his quarry. Also it occurred to Guy that the man might well double back to the barrack and relight the blaze, if his pursuer should allow himself to be lured far enough away. Running back, Guy went to the house and called forth Gray Dawn. The huge collie came bounding out eagerly, at the summons.

"You and I are going to mount guard tonight, Dawn," whispered Guy. "*Watch!*"

The trained watchdog needed no second bidding. Alert, tense, he set forth for his first round of the buildings. Guy stepped inside the house for his pistol and for his flashlight. Though he knew there was scant chance that the incendiary would return that same night, yet he wished to take no possible risk by negligence.

As he was going out again, Klyda called softly to him from within her room:

"Is anything the matter, Mr. Manell? I thought I heard you running. And then Gray Dawn ran out, too."

"Everything is all right," he heard himself answer, his throat contracted by his recent excitement. "Is your father comfortable?"

"Yes," said the girl. "I looked in on him, only a minute ago. He is still sound asleep. Good night."

"Good night," returned Manell, dizzily, as he made his way out of the house.

Seating himself on the porch, he began his long vigil. Dawn, returning from his patrol-round, curled up at his master's feet. So, for hours, sat the two, breaking their night's monotony, twice or thrice, by a perfunctory round of the buildings. As the east began to grow sickly yellow and the big white stars faded to mistily-seen points, Manell made his final round for the night. The ranch laborers would be stirring before long. There was no further need of vigilance. No marauder would risk detection at such an hour.

Guy took from his pocket his pad of paper-slips and a pencil. He wrote his foreman's name and a line instructing him to report at the house as soon as he was up. Folding the note and tying it to Dawn's collar, he said:

"Foreman, Dawn! *Foreman!*"

It was not the first nor the fiftieth time Manell had sent messages in this fashion to his foreman or to Sing. Dawn, like any collie trained to the task, always bore these straight to their destination, no matter what the distance. Guy knew the collie would gallop directly to the foreman's shack; and there he would scratch at the door until it should be opened. The bit of paper hanging from his shaggy throat would tell its own story.

Off bounded Gray Dawn. Manell settled back in his porch chair for a cat-nap, before it should be time for him to bathe and dress for the day. He was not minded to have more of these sleepless nights. Hence his note to the foreman. He had decided to tell the man of his adventure with the incendiary, and to have one of the best workers detailed as night guard of the buildings, along with Gray Dawn, until the scare should be over.

Guy was dead-tired. For two nights he had had no sleep. Now that there was no further need to stay on guard, his mind and body slumped. He fell into a heavy doze, his last waking thought being a hope that Dawn would come back quietly from his errand and not choose that time to stick his moist nose lovingly into the face of his slumbering master, nor to invite him to a romp.

He need not have worried. Dawn was not coming home with any undue quickness. The foreman had had a late evening at Santa Dereta and had not returned to his shack until two o'clock in the morning. He was sleeping, now, far too soundly and snorefully for the most imperative scratch at his front door to bring him back to wakefulness.

Dawn scratched loudly, four or five times. Then he circled the shack and came back and scratched again. His circumnavigation told him, through his uncannily keen nostrils, that the foreman had come in and had not since gone out. The distantly-heard snores of the sleeper confirmed the theory.

Dawn had been sent to deliver this note. Obviously, it was his job to stay as near as possible to the addressee of the note, until it could be delivered. Wherefore, after one more scratch at the scored panel of the door, he lay down on the steps to wait for the slumberer to come forth.

Guy Manell woke up wide, and with a start, instinctively aware that someone was watching him. This odd sense was reinforced by the approach of soft steps. He opened his eyes. The world around him was glorious with the rising of the sun. For a full hour he had been sleeping like the dead.

Coming toward him from the direction of the vineyards was a wiry figure. At a distance of fifty feet, Guy recognized the swarthy face and the inevitable black felt hat of Tawakwina, the Carlisle-graduate Shoshone Indian he had hired two days earlier.

The Shoshone's black eyes were fixed on him in a most intent stare. He was advancing rapidly, never once moving his keen gaze from his employer. Guy understood, now, why he had had the sensation of being stared at, as well as the origin of the fast-approaching tread. He sat up abruptly in his chair, with the subconscious aversion to being caught asleep which is the throwback trait of humans. The sudden gesture dislodged from his chest something that seemed to have been pinned carelessly to the front of his shirt. The thing fell into his lap.

Looking down, he saw his knees were covered by the crackling object. It was a twenty-by-twenty square of thick brown paper like the other warnings' stationery. Across it in the same sticky reddish fluid was the legend:

"Yu hav one (1) week to git out. If not gone then thare wil be no more warrning and the third (3d) bulet wit not miss and the third (3d) fire wil not go out and the nife that cut yur frends cattels throtes wil not mis yures. Yu have one (1) week to go."

His eye ran over the screed, in a single sweep. Then, instinctively, as the Indian came toward him, he crumpled the paper and hid it behind him in the deep chair, to keep it from the Shoshone's sight.

It occurred to Guy, now, that it must have been the unusual spectacle of a man sitting asleep with his whole chest covered by a sheet of brown paper, which had riveted the oncoming Indian's gaze so intently on him. Also that the fellow could not but be curious at seeing him hide the thing in such guilty haste.

But these conjectures did not interest him one-tenth as much as the stark miracle of the paper's presence on his chest. While he slept, someone had come up to him, too silently to awaken him, and had affixed the eccentrically-spelt notice to the front of his shirt.

It was humiliating — vexatious. It sent a throb of impotent anger through the man, as might a publicly-perpetrated practical joke. He had been made ridiculous.

He had kept such keen vigil that night! Yet, with perfect ease, he had been caught off-guard. Not even his dog had been there to protect him. Manell well knew that Gray Dawn would have permitted no one on earth to lay a hand on his sleeping master, nor to approach within reach of him. But Dawn was away. He himself had sent him.

(Dawn, by the way, at this moment was standing impatiently, while a tousle-headed and sleep-numbed foreman was taking from his collar the note written more than an hour earlier.)

Then, as the Shoshone paused respectfully at the foot of the porch steps, Manell accosted him with undue sharpness, venting some of his vexed self-contempt on the nearest human available.

"Well?" he demanded. "What do *you* want? I've given orders for you fellows to keep away from the house, unless you're sent for. What do you want? And what's that you've got there?"

For answer the Shoshone held forth a gnarled dark-brown twig, with roots at one end of it, from which hung crumbling lumps of earth. It was a young grape-vine, newly pulled up from the soil. Manell looked inquisitively at it. Before he could voice his query again, the Shoshone spoke.

"I did not know it was against orders to approach the house," said he. "I ask pardon. The need seemed to justify it. I came to work, just now, past the new five-acre vineyard we were planting yesterday and that the rest have been at work on for some days. I found this. I looked for the foreman. He was not out, yet. So I ventured to bring it here."

"Hey!" exclaimed the indignant Manell. "You pulled up one of my new Sultana plants by the roots and brought it here? What in blazes — ?"

"No, sir," was the unruffled answer. "It was lying at one side of the vineyard, with the earth still damp around its roots. I —"

"But why bring it here?" persisted Manell. "Why didn't you find where it had been uprooted and plant it again?"

"Because it would have been lonely, being the only one there," was the answer. "And I could not find where it had been uprooted from. You see, *all* the vines in that five acres have been uprooted, since we left work last night. And all except this one have been carried away. The soil looks also as if salt had been sown on it. If I did wrong in bringing this theft to your attention —"

But Manell was out of his chair and off the porch, and racing across the meadow toward the vineyards. He did not wait to hear the rest of the slowly spoken words. Nor did he pause until he came to the five-acre field where, only yesterday evening, most of the grayish alluvial soil had been symmetrically dotted with high-priced new Sultana vines.

Not a vine was left.

The field was empty. Everywhere it was trodden by flat surfaces, as though the despoilers had strapped shingles to their foot-soles to destroy any chance of telltale footprints. Men had worked long and fast, in the hours of darkness, to obliterate this promising young vineyard. But they had done their work well. Not a plant was to be seen anywhere in the upheaved surface of the tract. Salt was strewn, thickly, everywhere.

Manell turned around, dazed. Slowly and at a distance, Tawakwina was coming toward him from the direction of the house. Then Guy remembered he himself had raced hither, leaving in the porch chair the crumpled warning. It was highly possible that Tawakwina had stopped long enough to read the paper which had so interested him, before following to the despoiled vineyard. The thought made Guy the more brusque as he hailed the Shoshone.

"Chase to the foreman's shack!" commanded Manell. "Jump! Tell him what's happened and send him here. Quick!"

Chapter 17

When Guy returned to his cottage at last for breakfast, it was with the memory of a loudly blasphemous foreman and of a gaping clump of workers and of a useless search of the ranch for the costly young vines that had been torn up.

But Manell found to his surprise that he looked forward with more interest to his approaching breakfast with Klyda Graeme than to the chances of overhauling the mischievous disciple of sabotage who had ruined his new vineyard.

In vain, during the night's watch, had he tried to solve the problem of Saul Graeme's face, glimpsed by the fugitive flicker of match-light. Even so he had earlier given up the mystery of seeing Graeme's face vanishing into the chaparral, across from the ledge on Grudge Mountain, within a few seconds of the time he had seen Graeme sitting in front of his own shack, nearly six miles away, and of Old Man Negley's hailing of Saul.

"Outside of movies and dime novels," he told himself, "there is no such thing as a 'double' or a secret twin brother. Besides, Klyda said she had no living relatives except her father. As for doubles — well, the man who could 'double' that craglike extra-sized visage of his would be worth seeing. And — and yet, the old chap's leg is broken. I proved that. So did Doc Vreeland. And a man with a broken leg couldn't have gotten out of the house and all the way to the hay-barrack. It's a sure thing he couldn't have run like the wind as that firebug ran. He — There she is!"

He quickened his pace as he saw Klyda standing on the porch waiting for him. Wondrous pretty and dainty she was, in the clear morning light, with the flowering vines as a frame for her slender figure and highbred little face. The man's heart felt that same queer throb again, at sight of her. Again he marveled vexedly at the phenomenon.

Then he noted that she was holding in one hand the sheet of crumpled brown paper he had left in the chair. There was a cloud of worry in her dark eyes. He had not meant to trouble her with knowledge of this latest warning. He was sorry that she had found it and that it seemed to have added perceptibly to her uneasiness.

"How is Mr. Graeme?" he asked, as he came up.

"He had a bad night," she answered. "But he says he is lots comfortabler this morning. He isn't, of course. He must be in terrible pain. But he won't confess it. That's like Dad. Look!" she interrupted herself, holding out the crumpled paper. "Have you seen this?"

"Yes," he made answer. "But I wish *you* hadn't."

"Why?"

"Haven't you enough to bother you, already?"

"This doesn't 'bother' me," said Klyda. "It's the nearest approach to consolation any of us have had. Read it again. Don't you see it's a reprieve?"

"A — a what?" he asked, glancing over the scrawled words afresh.

"A reprieve. It says you have a week. That means there'll be nothing to molest you for at least seven days."

Guy thought of the demolished vineyard; but he said nothing.

"Don't you see?" she urged. "For a whole week we can set our wits to work, solving this. If we hit on a clue, in that time, we may be able to —"

"I see," he said, but with no enthusiasm.

"The police can discover something in that time, I'm sure," she went on.

Guy Manell knew too little of women to realize that this eager optimism, before breakfast, after a night of broken rest, spoke more glowingly for the girl's character and for the good luck of the man who should be so fortunate as to marry her than could a bookful of testimonials. All he knew was that she was disturbingly pretty, there in the sunlight, as she looked down at him. To check his impulse to stare at her in mute admiration, he tried to visualize the aspect of the Santa Dereta police, should he go to them with the statement that he and Graeme had been shot at with golden bullets and that he had seen a broken-legged man run like an athlete.

"I think," he said, slowly, "I think I'll play a lone hand in this game. The local police are fine. But this is a bit beyond police action, in its present shape. Shall we have breakfast?"

"You're not going to 'play a lone hand'!" she denied in a flash of white-hot spirit. "My father has been wounded. Our home has been burned down. Our horses and our cow have been killed. Everything we own has been destroyed. Except the one trunk and valise that Dad was able to get out of the shack before it burned down. I am not going to sit still and let you take the time and the risk of hunting all alone for the criminals who did that. I am going to help. And you are going to let me help. You *are!* Promise you will. *Say* so!"

"Yes," he answered, slowly, though he said it as if humoring a child. "Yes, I promise. Now let's eat."

That pleasant breakfast together, on the breezy veranda, among the flowers, with Gray Dawn and the Reverend Wilberforce as eagerly self-invited guests, was the one bright spot in a dull day. Guy was kept busy, in the search for the stolen vines. Then he had to drive across to Santa Dereta to telegraph for another consignment, on the chance it might arrive before the brief planting season should end. There were a score of other details that ate up his day, to no satisfaction to himself and to no visible profit to his ranch.

Klyda's own day was little less annoying. Her

father was suffering greatly. Fever had set in. Dr. Vreeland, on his noonday call, was less professionally cheerful than on the day before. Not understanding that the second day of a case of fracture is nearly always far more painful and disturbing than the first, Klyda worried keenly. She spent the entire day and evening at Graeme's bedside, even taking her meals there.

Thus, Guy saw practically nothing of her. Disgruntled, and sharing not at all in her solicitude for the sufferer, he sulked on the porch, with Dawn at his feet, for an hour after supper. Then he went to bed.

He had arranged for a trusty worker to patrol the home ranch that night, and for the big collie to act as auxiliary guard. Between the two, nothing was likely to go amiss; especially as the foreman, horrified at the tale of attempted incendiarism, vowed to share the patrol at least twice during the night.

Thus, Guy could afford to sleep the sleep of utter exhaustion. Nor did he wake until just before daybreak. Then, refreshed, he went out into the dim-lit world, to find that no disturbance of any kind had marked the night. It was too early to start his men to work for the day. Klyda was still asleep. Instinctively his mind went back to Grudge Mountain and to the mystery of the choked groove. Its baffling lure was upon him at once.

Half-guiltily, he turned his footsteps toward the valley-mouth. Gray Dawn bounded along, far in advance. But Guy whistled back the dog, and bade him go home. While the night had passed safely, yet day had not fairly broken. It might be that some further sabotage attempt would be made in the two hours before the men should be astir.

"Back, Dawn!" he commanded. *"Watch!"*

Unwillingly the big collie obeyed. Guy strode on, with growing curiosity as to what miraculous change might have befallen the groove and the ledge during his absence. Anything seemed possible, now, in that sinister spot.

Yes, anything seemed possible. Yet with a start Manell observed the first outstanding sight that met his eye as he neared the mountain-foot. He rounded the bend in the trail and came out almost directly under the smaller and lower ledge of Grudge Mountain. At a point where this ledge jutted out over a perpendicular cliff of mountain-wall, a human figure was dangling from the brink of the platform.

Guy blinked. He looked more closely, in the gray light. Now he saw the figure was a man's, dressed as a laborer. The man evidently had been walking along the ledge when, passing too near the verge, his foot had slipped on the dew-slimed rock and he had fallen. In falling, he had grasped a dwarf evergreen sapling which had found precarious roothold in the soil of a rock-fault. To this he was clinging. His body dangled out over the precipice; the shallowly planted evergreen bent farther outward under his wriggling weight at every frantic struggle to raise himself.

As Guy looked, the imperilled man seemed to recognize that any further strain might tear the sapling free from its precarious moorings and send it and its human burden crashing to the pointed boulders on the ground far below. For he ceased to strive; and he fixed his eyes on the gradually loosening roots of the treelet.

Guy stood for an instant, staring up at him. Then, dim as was the light, he recognized the victim. It was his own Shoshone laborer, Tawakwina.

How the Indian had climbed to the ledge was incomprehensible, until Manell bethought him of the barely scalable strip of rock at its far end. But why a man should risk more than even chances of death by attempting so fearfully hazardous a climb, he could not understand. Especially as there seemed nothing on the bleak ledge to justify the peril of an ascent.

Still, the fact remained that Tawakwina had climbed to the ledge and, while walking along it, had slipped over the brink. There he hung. Momentarily, the sapling bent more and more outward, as the roots, one by one, snapped or were torn from their rock-cracks.

Tawakwina hung moveless, now. No sound escaped his gray-white lips. With the stoic calm of his race, he had resigned himself to the inevitable. Stolidly he was awaiting the fall which must kill him.

The man's pluck appealed strongly to Manell. Without weighing the long chances against success in his own mad plan, he set off at a run for the part of the cliff, some distance beyond, where rock-faults and an occasional bush might possibly lend foot- or hand-hold to a light and agile climber who could keep his head.

The odds were pitiably great against the success of such an attempt. Yet the Shoshone's death was certain, unless Guy could not only make his way to the ledge, but could do so before the sapling should give way completely under Tawakwina's weight.

Thus, as fast as his feet could carry him, Manell raced for the cliff-corner. As he ran, he reflected that probably he could climb any wall which this older and less athletic Indian had been able to ascend. The thought gave him fresh hope.

Along the few remaining rods of trail he sped. But, midway, he came to a stop. Great as was his need for haste, a most undramatic object in the center of the path had arrested his flight.

There lay a small and stubby grapevine, with dry dirt still sticking to its roots. No need for a second glance to tell Guy the nature and origin of this uprooted vine. It was one of the countless stolen plants from his five-acre Sultana vineyard — one of the hundreds of plants which so mysteriously had disappeared.

Here it lay, withering in the trail, far from the scene of theft. The despoilers of the vineyard had passed this way with their booty and, carelessly, had let fall this one plant.

Chapter 18

But the trail led only to Grudge Mountain and thence around, by circuitous and difficult route, to a taproot of the Ridge Road. It seemed impossible that the thieves would have taken such a uselessly long and out-of-the-way trip, to carry off their plunder. Moreover, there were no vineyards in this direction, for many miles; nor any ranches. What sense was there in bearing the stolen plants through the Grudge Mountain pass?

For a second at most did Guy pause, to gaze in astonishment at the twist of stem and root. Then, once more he was running. Theft clues could wait. A human life could not.

He reached the foot of the precipitous climb. Then he stopped once more, this time to kick off his moccasins and to toss aside his coat. Then he called:

"Hang on, Tawakwina! I'll be there in a minute. Keep still! Don't move!"

The Indian's black eyes — stolid with the look of approaching death — turned downward upon Manell at sound of the hail. But he gave no other sign. Nor did he stir. His swarthy face was a death-mask.

Guy began his all-perilous climb. Though every sense and every atom of brain and strength

158

were needed for the ascent, he noted subconsciously an odd fact! More than one twiglike plant came away in his hand, as he sought to test its ability to bear his weight. Leaves and small branches snapped.

Yet, looking upward, he could see no sign that the foliage above him had been disturbed or crushed in any way by the ascent of Tawakwina, who, obviously, must have come up to the ledge by this one remotely passable way. There was not a sign that anyone had climbed the face of the plant-starred cliff ahead of Manell.

Even this incongruity could not absorb Guy's attention, as he squirmed his way upward. He was playing with death; and the odds were all against him. It was no time to wonder about anything, except about his own decreasing chances of reaching the ledge before Tawakwina should fall, or indeed before he himself should be sent toppling down, by some misstep.

Deftly he chose each inequality of the rock wall, for toes or fingers to cling to. Cautiously, he tested and used each outthrusting plant that could bear a portion of his weight. With the skilled balance of a pugilist, he adjusted that weight of his, to suit every shift of posture and to bear as lightly as possible on the stem or crumbling fissure which just then might happen to be supporting it.

Once, with the fingers of his left hand hooked in a rift of the wall, he reached upward and lifted himself by a staunch-looking greasewood stump which grew just above. He let go of the fissure which his toes had gripped. The greasewood snapped, just as he put his weight on it.

Down lurched Guy, hanging for a moment by the fingers of his left hand to the rift he had almost released; his legs and his body were swinging in space, his toes clawing blindly for the fissure which they had just quitted.

By rare luck his foot touched and grasped the fissure. He regained his lost equilibrium. Panting, he hugged the face of the cliff; while he looked for the next possible means of helping himself upward.

A less sturdy-looking, but more reliable, bush was barely in reach, if he should stand on tiptoe in the fissure and raise his free arm to it. This he caught and tested, worming his way up till his toe was in the rift that had supported his fingers.

So, yard by yard, and resisting the craving to look at the widening depth below him, he swarmed upward. At times, the going was almost easy. During these intervals he attained the speed of a cat. Again, the way seemed impassable, and he must needs flirt with death for every inch of headway.

He could not remember when he had not been crawling thus between earth and sky; nor could he look forward to any time when he should not still be doing so. As a matter of fact, the fearsome ascent occupied little more than a minute in all. But the strain on nerve and muscle sickened him.

When at last the brink of the ledge was within reach, he needed all his remaining powers of will and of body to draw himself up over it and onto the safety of the ledge.

There, for an instant, he lay panting, trying to conquer the dizziness which threatened to overmaster him. Then he got to his feet. But his first step was the step of a drunkard. For he lurched heavily on his overstrained legs and would have fallen, if he had not thrown out both hands against a boulder which lay at the back of the ledge, supported against the wall of the mountain.

So dizzy was he that this rock seemed actually to sway sideways under his hands.

By a mighty effort of will-power he was himself once more; at least to the extent of remembering Tawakwina's dire peril and of forcing himself to the final and crowning part of his rescue-quest.

Staggering across to the spot where Tawakwina's boot-marks showed the manner of his slipping from the wet ledge, Guy threw himself face downward and peered over. A foot or so beneath him hung the Shoshone, still gripping the trunk of the sapling.

In another second or two he and the sapling would have been hurtling together toward the rock-teeth far below. For, even as Manell reached downward, the last root snapped noisily and the little tree fell out into space.

It was touch-and-go. But, as the root broke, Manell's down-darting hands seized Tawakwina's wrists. There was a wrench. The Shoshone's full weight hung limp in his rescuer's grip. Guy felt his own braced body slipping outward along the grease-slippery ledge, as the augmented weight pulled it.

Then, with a heave that called for every atom of muscular power left to him, he slung the Indian upward and sideways. The Shoshone's toe came over the brink. Booted as it was, it clung to the slight vantage-hold and helped to draw up the rest of his hanging body. A dual heave and a scramble; and Tawakwina was rolling over, in safety, on the ledge.

Gasping, Manell got up and surveyed the prostrate Indian. His own nerve was none too steady. To hide his sick reaction, he said, lightly:

"Well, my aborigine friend, now that we're here, we're here. But I'm blest if I know how we're going to get down again. I wouldn't go back the way I came, for a million dollars. Got any suggestions to offer?"

Tawakwina made no reply. He was lying on his face, where he had rolled when he came up over the ledge. That final effort had been too much for him. Terror and shock and relief had combined to make him swoon.

Manell turned him over on his back. There was no water wherewith to revive him. Guy tore open the neck and breast of the man's calico shirt, to give his chest to the air. The action caused something to fall out of the breast of the shirt — something which had been hidden in a tiny inside pocket of the garment. It fell to the ledge beside him. Guy picked it up.

The thing was an image, apparently of a heathen goddess; it was wrought with an infinite artistry, far foreign to clumsy Indian workmanship. Worn and blurred with vast age, it was nevertheless indescribably exquisite in form and design.

Incidentally, it was of solid gold.

With an inexplicable feeling of having pried into another's religious secrets, Guy stuck the image back into its place. The next moment, Tawakwina's eyes opened. With a galvanic effort he sat up and stared dully around him.

The chilliness of his chest seemed to tell him his shirt was open. Snakelike in quickness, his hand sought the inner pocket where reposed the golden image. Finding it safe, his hand continued the same gesture by buttoning his shirt, as though that were the sole cause for the rapid motion of his fingers toward his chest.

Then, midway of this simple procedure, he shuddered violently. Memory was coming back upon him, with a rush. He made as though to struggle to his feet.

"Take it easy!" counseled Guy. "You have had a nasty twist. Stay still, till you get better hold of yourself. It'll be time enough then for us to figure how to get out of this. We —"

With a strangled cry, Tawakwina sprang up. Before Manell could guess his purpose, he flung himself on his knees on the rocky ledge in front of Guy, declaiming brokenly a flood of words in his native Shoshone dialect.

He seemed to be intoning some ritual, his guttural voice rising and sinking in rhythmic sequence, his every tone fraught with ardent reverence.

It was to Manell and not to a deity that he chanted his strange ritual. Before the amazed rancher found speech to interrupt or to ask the meaning of the weird intoning, Tawakwina finished the performance by stooping suddenly lower, and placing Manell's stockinged right foot on his bowed neck.

"Hold on there!" ordered Guy, embarrassed. "Stop that! What sort of foolery are you going through, anyhow? I —"

Something whizzed downward past Manell's head. A fist-sized rock smote the ledge with terrific force. Guy looked up.

"The start of a landslide," he said. "Let's get closer to the wall. If that thing had hit one of us —"

"Yes!" cried Tawakwina, with sudden vehemence, his own eyes lifted in blank terror. "Back to the wall, sir! Quickly!"

He seized Manell and thrust him backward toward the shelter of the mountainside, striving to interpose himself between the other man and any further rock that might fall. But, on the same instant, a second stone dropped from somewhere above. The Shoshone cried out and tried to shove Guy out of its path. He was too late.

The stone missed the crown of Manell's hatless skull. But it smote glancingly against the side of his head.

The world went black. Guy pitched to the ledge floor, inert and moveless. In his ears, as he fell, seemed to sound a giant voice, rage-shaken and horrible, which answered Tawakwina's scream of fright.

Chapter 19

With his head ringing and racked and still echoing with the Shoshone's cry and with the great raging voice answering it, Manell opened his eyes.

Apparently, he was lying where he had fallen when the rock had smitten him senseless to the ledge floor. Apparently, too, the Indian was still leaning above him, as if to act as a human shield against any further hurtling stones.

For Guy was stretched out on his back and someone was bending above him. His dazed senses could not at first make out his surroundings with any distinctness. Nor had he the faintest desire to. For his head was torturing him; and the light was a torment to his bloodshot eyes.

So he let fall his tired lids, content to rest as he was, until surcease of pain and a clearing of intelligence should prompt him to take up the burden of life again.

Meantime, it was vaguely pleasant to be ministered to, as Tawakwina was now ministering to him. The Indian was stroking the pain-torn forehead, with a wondrous light and magnetic touch — a touch that soothed the hurt and sent a drowsy feeling of wellbeing through the stricken rancher. He hated to be pawed by any

166

man. Always he had loathed it. Yet now —

The light hand was lifted; and Guy wished dully for a renewal of the magic touch. Strange that an uncouth-looking Shoshone should have such marvelously healing fingers! Strange that Guy himself should tolerate their contact! He could not understand it.

A minute more, and the hand was on his forehead again. This time, it was bathing the hot flesh with cool water. The impossibility of the happening lifted Manell from his apathy. There was no water on the ledge, except what the night's dew had deposited on it. Surely there was not enough of that to soak a handkerchief as completely as this kerchief which sponged his brow.

The rousing of Guy's mind from its daze made him now aware that his entire head was swathed in a wet cloth — a cloth whose coolness was as balm to the intolerable ache. Where did all that water come from? Every southern California ranchman thinks in terms of water. For on water depends his livelihood. If there were a hidden spring on the ledge —

Manell opened his eyes once more, this time focusing his blurred gaze, instead of letting it stay blank.

He was in the little living-room of his own cottage in Friendly Valley, the room into which he had had a cot moved when he gave up his bedroom to Saul Graeme. On this cot he was lying, full-dressed except for coat and moccasins. He recalled now that he had cast these aside when he began his climb to the ledge.

Above him leaned Klyda Graeme, her flower-face drawn and frightened.

How he came to be in his own living-room — how this girl, instead of the rescued Shoshone, chanced to be tending him — he neither knew nor cared. Enough that she was with him, and that her gentle hand was on his forehead. He forced his lips into a feeble grin as he looked up at her.

"*Oh!*" sighed the girl in utter relief. "You know me! You know me, at last! Every time your eyes have opened, they were so blind, so dreadfully dead! But now you *do* know me!"

She spoke impulsively, more to herself than to him. But he made answer in a husky whisper that seemed to him to come from miles away:

"Of course, I know you. Why shouldn't I? There isn't — there isn't anyone else in the world like you."

She reddened; and he wondered vaguely how he had chanced to babble such an idiotic thing. Recovering herself she admonished him:

"You mustn't talk. You must lie still. Try to sleep. I have sent your foreman over to Santa Dereta for Dr. Vreeland. He ought to be here before now. Till he comes, you must rest. Shut your eyes. Don't speak. It's bad for you to exert yourself."

Dazedly he obeyed. The brief effort of answering her, and even of listening to her, had increased the pain in his head. He was well content to shut his eyes again and to lie there quietly while she smoothed his aching forehead.

But his swoon was past. Nor could he sink back into oblivion as before. His mind, through the mist of pain, would not cease again from functioning. By no volition of his own, he found his thoughts straying back to the scene of his before-sunrise adventure. Bit by bit, memory pieced into a complete fabric the fragmentary recollections of his journey to Grudge Mountain: the finding of the vine in the trail; Tawakwina's helpless body swinging out over space from the ever-weakening sapling; his own hazardous climb of the all-but-unscalable cliff and his rescue of the Shoshone in the very nick of time; the finding of the exquisitely-wrought golden image; the Indian's odd chant and obeisance to him and the placing of his foot on Tawakwina's neck; then the down-whizzing stone that so narrowly had missed him and the ensuing stone which had not missed him; the real voice and the imagined giant voice that smote upon his ear as he tumbled senseless.

He remembered it all, by degrees. And the memory was turbulent enough. But from remembering, his mind drifted to conjecture.

He and Tawakwina had been alone on the ledge, much more than a hundred feet above ground. The only way up or down was by that perilous climb of the cliff's rugged face. It had taken all his own prowess to ascend the cliff; and it had been done at imminent life-risk.

Manifestly, it was impossible that Tawakwina had carried him to earth along that same precipitous route. No mortal could have made the descent with a twenty-pound infant in his arms or tied to his back, to say nothing of a hundred-and-eighty-pound man who was unconscious.

It could not have been done. There was no question about that. Yet here he was, now, in his own home. Somehow, he had been brought down from the ledge and then he had been transported over rough ground to Friendly Valley. How had it been achieved? The longer Guy thought about it, the more perplexed he became.

Then it occurred to him that Tawakwina had undoubtedly called for help and his cries had been heard by some passing hiker or prospector or bindle stiff. A rope must have been gotten up in some way to the ledge and his inert body lowered by Tawakwina, and thence borne home.

Yes, that was the only sane solution. Yet Manell was resolved to confirm it. He opened his heavy eyes again, looking up into the little face that bent so anxiously above him.

"How — how did I get here?" he forced himself to ask; every word was a physical and mental effort.

"Hush!" she bade him, gently. "You mustn't talk."

In his weakened and nerveless condition he was as fretfully persistent as a sick boy.

"Tell me!" he begged, frowning with the effort the words cost him.

"If I tell you the little I know," said Klyda, speaking as might a mother who coaxes her baby to slumber, "will you promise to be still and try to rest?"

He nodded assent. It seemed easier to nod than to speak. But the motion sent a whirlwind of pain through his head.

"And you won't talk any more or ask any more questions, till Dr. Vreeland gets here?" she insisted.

"No," he croaked, judging rightly this time that words were less agonizing than headshakes.

"Sing had let Gray Dawn into the house, when he got up," she began. "I woke early, too. I had just finished dressing, when I heard Dawn snarling and tearing at the front door, to get out. He was terribly excited. I opened the door. You were lying on the porch. You were unconscious; and there was that great bruise on the side of your head. Nobody else was in sight. But Dawn kept rushing up and down and in circles, snarling and growling. First he would dart off, on some scent. Then he'd gallop back and lick your face and whimper. I sent Sing for the foreman and some of the men; and they carried you in here and went for the doctor. That was a whole hour ago." She broke off in distress. "Surely Dr. Vreeland ought to be here. I sent word for him to hurry as fast as he could. Oh, I was afraid you were — afraid you were —"

A stifled sob choked her fast-whispered words. Manell longed to comfort her, to reassure her, in some way. But her tidings had set his brain awhirl, once more.

Then a rescue party had not gotten a rope to the ledge and had him lowered by Tawakwina and borne him home? In some utterly impossible manner, he had been wafted from the ledge to his own doorway; and none had seen him brought hither.

If Tawakwina had hit upon means of getting him to earth and had carried him all the way home, the Shoshone would scarce have dumped him on the porch, after taking so much trouble to get him there; nor would he have strolled off and left him, stricken and senseless, to be found by chance. Nor would any normal mortal have done such a thing.

An enemy, if he had one, would not have gone to the exertion and the risk of bringing him, unharmed, to the cottage. No, the puzzle could not be solved by any hypothesis. The one fact remained that there must be other ways of reaching and leaving that lower ledge, than by climbing the precipitous rock-face. The rest was a muddle.

While he was still moiling over the tangled theme, a car stopped at the gate. Klyda glanced out of the window; then she ran from the room. A minute later she came back with Dr. Vreeland.

Followed a painful examination of the bruised head, and the terse verdict that the injury had not caused fracture. There had been a brief concussion of the brain. Nothing worse.

As he dressed the bruise and gave directions to Klyda, the physician interrupted himself in his task, to inquire:

"Got any idea how this happened? Miss Graeme tells me she found you on your doorstep, knocked out."

Guy thought, for a moment. Thinking was a less agonizing labor, every minute, now. Moreover, the pain, while still torturing him, was more bearable. Vreeland was a good surgeon and a better physician. But many rural doctors have a love for gossip. Manell did not relish the idea of his adventure serving in garbled form as ranch talk for a radius of twenty miles.

"I went up beyond the mouth of the valley," he said, heavily. "I must have hit my head on a rock, while I was climbing that bunch of boulders. The footing is pretty bad, you know. Especially where I was. Probably I had enough subconscious sense to stagger back as far as my own porch, before I collapsed. I —"

"H'm!" commented the doctor. "Not a bad lie, for a chap whose wits are still scattered."

Guy tried to look righteously indignant. The attempt hurt his sore head.

"There!" soothed Vreeland. "Don't get riled. It's nobody's business but your own. One story is as good as another. Yours sounds all right. Only it couldn't happen. People don't walk a mile over broken ground with concussion of the brain. Keep that in mind, if you're tempted to spring the same yarn on some other doctor. It will go down all right with a layman."

"I tell you, I —"

"So you said. Now, Miss Graeme, we'll take a look at your father. This boy here will be as good as new by tomorrow, except for a mighty sore bump on his sconce. Lucky the blow fell on his skull, instead of some less solid part of him. Lie still, Manell, for the rest of the day. Miss Graeme will see the dressings are renewed and kept damp. Get some sleep. You'll feel like another man when you wake up. I'll be in, tomorrow, to see Mr. Graeme. You'll be all right by then."

As the doctor and Klyda passed out of the room, Guy found himself muttering:

"Yes, there must be some other way of getting to that ledge. More than that, there must be some way of getting to parts of the mountain above it. Those two stones never fell where they did, from chance. The first one may have landed alongside me, by accident. But Tawakwina had pushed me back, a good six feet, when the second one hit me. Landslides don't 'place their hits' with stones, as accurately as all that. There was someone farther up the mountain who was pelting me. Perhaps the same man who pelted Saul Graeme, when he tried to climb up the other side, that day. The mountain-face looks like a straight wall of rock. But it must be hollow — in places, anyhow. Only — only — how in blue blazes do the people in the secret manage to get up inside there? — Who are they and how do they get there?"

Upon him crept the memory of the gigantic ice-cold hand he had gripped in the darkness of the upper ledge's cavern, and of the great raging voice.

"Maybe I was a loud-mouthed fool to bawl that challenge up to them, whoever they are," he told himself. "But it *goes!* Nobody's going to give me a bugaboo scare like that and then try to brain me with stones — and get away with it."

Chapter 20

At the resolve, he felt the old unreasoning anger and determination sweep across him, banishing for the moment the realization that he was laid up with a scourgingly sore head and a nauseating dizziness.

"I'll find out the secret, whatever it turns out to be!" he fumed impotently. "And I've a hunch I'll find one end of it is tied up in some way with this golden bullet buncombe and the comic opera warnings and the rest of the hodgepodge that has been piling on us."

His foreman passed the open window.

"Send Tawakwina to me," called Guy.

"He didn't show up today, Boss," answered the man. "Sent me a note by a kid, just now, that he's quitting. Says he's leaving the state. Didn't even ask for his pay. . . . How's the head feeling now? Any better?"

By early afternoon, Manell was so much himself again that he defied Klyda's commands to lie still. He insisted on going out to the veranda, where she made him vastly comfortable in his big chair.

"It's lot of fun to play invalid," he assured her. "If I were well, you know you'd never waste so much of your time in taking beautiful care of me. Never since my mother died has any woman smoothed a pillow and put it behind my head when I was sick. I'll wake up presently and find it's all a gorgeous dream."

She smiled down at him in shy appreciation of his praise. Then she said:

"I wish we could wake up and find the rest of it is a dream, too."

"With luck," he made cryptic reply, "perhaps we can keep the other dream from coming true. I have an idea — perhaps it's a crazy one — that I can get hold of a clue to all this, as soon as I'm on my feet again. And that'll be by tomorrow. You heard what Doc told me about a crack on the head, like this? He said if the skull isn't fractured or the brain put out of business, it's the quickest part of the body to recover. Why, football-players and prizefighters get knocked cold; and in ten minutes they're as good as ever! Outdoor hustling has put me in almost as good condition as they are. I used to be a boxer, by the way, and a wrestler, too. I won a couple of medals for ama-teur glove-and-mat-work, just before I came out here. Well, if fighters can get over a knockout in no time, so can I. The old head has stopped banging and now it's only sore. I'm not half as wobbly as I was, either. So you're not to worry over me, any longer. I was a football man, too, at —"

The chug and rattle of a car at the gate drowned his words. He looked up to see Old

Man Negley lowering himself gruntingly from his antique runabout.

"What rotten luck!" complained Guy, under his breath. "Someone is always throwing a handful of sawdust into my beer."

"I ought to be sitting with Dad, anyhow," said Klyda. "Don't let yourself get tired and don't talk too much."

She slipped into the house, leaving him to meet his guest with what cordiality he could muster.

"Hello, there!" wheezed Old Man Negley, as he stumped up the steps. "I met Doc Vreeland. Over at Santa Dereta. He told me you'd been breaking rock. With your skull. Kind of paltry amusement for a grown man, hey? Thought I'd run over. To see how you're getting on."

He shook his host's unresponsive hand, then seated himself rheumatically in the veranda's only other chair.

"Have a cigar?" proffered Guy.

The old man took the cigar. He crushed it deftly between his withered palms and stuffed the handful of broken tobacco into his mouth.

"Thanks," he mumbled, as he reduced the shattered particles to a quid, and began to chew ruminatively. "This is a good eating-cigar. As good as I've bit into in a month. Better'n the cooking cigars at Santa Dereta. How'd you hurt your head?"

"Oh," said Guy, with elaborate carelessness, "I got to thinking over what you told me about the gold in these mountains; and I went prospecting. A stray pebble, from up somewhere, tried to start a landslide; and it bumped off of my bean as it came down."

"Huh!" snorted Old Man Negley. "Another gold-idiot! Something about this California air sets folks to gold-chasing. The real gold is in the crops. Just begging to be coined into cash. Besides, I never told you there was gold in these mountains. All I said was that a lying Injun sprung a wild-goose yarn. In our camp, up near Calaveras. About a secret hoard of gold a prehistoric race had hid hereabouts. We were silly. Being hard up and being dosed with yarns of California gold. A bunch of us came down here to prospect. And not one of us ever got a sight nor smell of gold. So much for *that* joke!"

"Just what did the Indian tell you people?" asked Manell, still trying to speak with no show of interest. "Was it the good old wheeze about the Lost Mine; or what?"

"Nope," replied Old Man Negley. "We were pretty gullible. But none of us would have been fools enough to be taken in by that. Not that white-whiskered spiel about the Lost Mine. That was a Dead One, even in those days. The Lost Mine was. I'm told it still catches eastern suckers, now and then. But it's dead, out here. Dead as the Widow's Son. Nope, this was a fancier story than that. The Injun claimed to have been kicked out of some tribe or clan. Or some fam'ly whose head man had inherited the secret.

179

He was sore on his crowd for banishing him. He wanted to get back at 'em. By blowing their holy secret. So much of it as he'd picked up from a word here and there. It wasn't much, at that. And the whole tale was a fancy lie. But it was good enough for us. To pry us loose from our jobs and bring us down here."

"Did the Indian come here, too?"

"Yep. We coaxed him to act as our guide. Promised to protect him from his own people, too. In case they didn't like his coming back and blowing the treasure-secret. He believed us. Injuns in those days still had a way — some of 'em — of believing white men. A lot of good it did him! He had the same run of luck that you had. Him and Sim Zabriskie of Pompton, N.J., set out. Early the morning after we got here. They set out, secret, to climb Grudge Mountain. They got mixed up in a baby landslide. We found 'em both, next day. Down under one of the ledges. With their heads stove in. And a lot of loose stones lying around them. After that, we had to play out our fourflush hand. Without any tips from the Injun. Never got a look-in at the gold. Why? Because there wasn't any. No more than there was in the Mexican days. Days when the Greasers heard the same yarn and tried to find the stuff."

"But there may have been prehistoric people here, once," suggested Guy. "And if there were —"

"Not any race here with enough civilization or

180

brains to lay up a treasure-house of gold," scoffed Negley. "There would be traces of them. Just as there are in Arizona and Yucatan. And the mound-builder country. Nary a trace of anything. More than a couple of centuries old. Not in this ruck of egregious old mountains. Nope. The whole thing was a sell. How's that new Sultana vineyard of yours coming on?"

Manell answered at random. His mind was afire with the narrative he had heard. The Indian and one of the explorers had been slain by the same kind of stone-bombardment that had so nearly killed him. They and himself — more than fifty years apart in time — had been stoned from a mysterious invisible spot on or in Grudge Mountain, as they attempted to scale it.

The Negley Indian had known the general whereabouts of the hoard. He had been leading his white companion, the North Jerseyman, Sim Zabriskie, toward it, when the mystic guardians of the treasure had stopped his quest and his life.

Again flared up within Manell that ever-smouldering resolve to wrest from the mountain its age-old secret, and to show the keepers of the hoard that they could not scare him away.

Now, thinking back, he recalled that the golden bullet and the first warning had followed his own earliest attempt to explore the ridge, in his water-hunt. The Graemes had climbed the ledge — apparently for the same purpose as had he. The warnings, and then the destruction of their home and their livestock, and the attempted killing of Saul Graeme, had followed almost instantly.

Yes, the guardians of the mountain were as murderously zealous in the protecting of their secret as they had been a half-century ago — and as they had been many years before that, when Santa Ana's lieutenant had fallen to death among the rocks, as the result of a mysteriously severed climbing-rope.

With a start Guy noted that Old Man Negley was eying him in inquiry.

"I asked you," the old chap was saying, "what's the name of that big feller I met here. The one with the all-fired pretty girl. The one I miscalled Saul Graeme?"

"His name," said Manell, "is just that. Saul Graeme."

Stiffly in evident hot offence, Old Man Negley got to his feet and started for his car. Over his shoulder, as he went, he said, acidly:

"If you think it's funny to make small of a man old enough to be your granther — just because my mind once happened to slip a cog, for a second — you've got a bum idea of a joke. Saul Graeme'd be near a hundred. If he was alive. I know that. Even if my mind did trip me up, just once. There's no call for you to insult me. Not when I ask you a civil question."

Refusing to listen to any word of explanation, Negley got painfully into his car and wheezed away, without so much as a backward look.

Guy sank back, deep in his chair, aquiver with

excitement. Added now to his angry resolution to balk the unknown forces which had assailed him, was the strange lust for gold.

And this primal passion lurks in the swamps at the base of every human brain. It is as much of an overmastering emotion as are love and hate and hunger and thirst. To sate it, a thousand wars have been waged and a hundred conquests made. California owes her birth to it. So does many another state.

It is not the mere desire for wealth. It is also the lure of the actual metal itself — the lure that drove men from home and comfort in 1849, to face famine and death and untold hardship in the unknown West — the lure which still keeps thousands of Northern California prospectors poor and ever on the move.

"The bullets were pure gold," muttered Guy. "So was Tawakwina's amulet. Where did that gold come from? It is hidden somewhere in Grudge Mountain. It is guarded by unseen creatures who murder and burn, to protect their secret. And — and by a Giant. By at least *one* Giant. Perhaps there are other Giants, too. That isn't any more ridiculous than the one I proved is there. Those same creatures were guarding it in Santa Ana's time and they've been guarding it ever since. I'm — I'm going back, for another try."

Chapter 21

Forgetting his dizzy weakness and his hurt head, he got up and tiptoed stealthily down the steps, lest his departure be heard by Klyda and she call him back.

Gray Dawn leaped up in joyous anticipation of a walk — a canine urge nearly as strong in its way as is the primal gold-lust in man — the urge which makes a tired dog leave his cozy rug in front of the fireplace, and dance with joy at prospect of accompanying his master for a stroll through rain or sleet.

This time Guy did not send his dog home. He needed Dawn for an experiment whose details had flashed into his mind. The collie hated the scent or sight of an Indian. He had growled furiously at the Shoshone. Manell planned to take him to the base of the lower ledge and let him range until he should strike Tawakwina's trail.

The Indian must have come to earth from the ledge, at some point near the mountain-foot, after Guy had been knocked senseless. He must have done so in order to send the note to the foreman saying he was not coming back to work. Very good. Dawn could be trusted to find the trail, and to cast back along it to its inception, wherever that might chance to be.

But the collie did even better than Guy had dared hope. Scarce had Manell and Gray Dawn reached the valley-mouth when Dawn sniffed the air, suspiciously. Then he dropped his questing muzzle to the ground. After a few confused circlings, he found the scent he wanted. Yet, as if remembering Guy's previous scoldings for his behavior toward Indians, he glanced back guiltily toward his master.

"Good boy!" approved Manell, pointing encouragingly. "Go ahead!"

The collie needed no further permission. Nose to ground he set off at a canter. Guy, still tottery in the legs, followed as best he could, over the broken ground. He understood. The dog had picked up Tawakwina's trail where the Indian had debauched into Friendly Valley from the direction of Grudge Mountain; and he was following it back to its source.

Evidently then it had been Tawakwina — alone or with help — who had carried Manell home that morning. This, too, would account for Dawn's snarling and tearing at the door to get out, as Klyda had described. He had caught the loathed scent of an Indian at his master's very doorway.

"He's following it, straight to Grudge Mountain!" exulted Guy, forgetting his own weakness in the zest of the pursuit. "When he stops, it'll be at the place where Tawakwina left the mountainside — whether he climbed down where I climbed up or whether he got down by some secret way."

Breathing heavily, Manell clambered over rocks and trotted along paths, after the collie. Once or twice, he was forced to call to Gray Dawn to stop and wait for him to come up; then putting the dog once more upon the scent.

Dawn was enjoying the hunt, tremendously. That he was making such a palpable hit with his worshipped master added fiftyfold to his zeal.

Thus, the two came at last to the bend of the trail whence that morning Guy had seen the Shoshone dangling from the lower ledge.

Sunset was striking the upper half of the loftily grim mountain, smearing its drab face with fiery red. But here at the base, the shadows were already beginning to lie darkly.

"There's one comfort, Dawn, old man," Guy informed the eager dog. "After the rap they gave my head this morning they won't be on the lookout for me to hike back here for more, on the very same day. That makes it a little bit less insane for me to come bungling in search of trouble, without so much as a gun or even a club. I —"

He stopped in stupid surprise.

For the nosing dog, too, had stopped. He had stopped short at the base of the cliff. Not at the spot where broken branches and crushed leaves still marked the scramble of Guy Manell to the ledge, twelve hours earlier, but at the most precipitate and unscalable stretch of perpendicular wall.

Here, from one or two strewn boulders at the

base, the precipice rock arose sheer for more than a hundred feet, without a break. Nobody, unpossessed of wings or of the suction paws of a fly, could have mounted that straight gray wall.

The anticlimax of his long and fast trip from Friendly Valley proved too much for Guy's overstrained strength. Dizziness deepened the growing shadows of the trail. Yet, bracing himself, and concluding that Tawakwina had merely paused there on his way, he bade the dog go on.

Gray Dawn ceased from sniffing around the bottom of a cliff-base boulder and obediently circled the surrounding ground. But midway in his circling he caught again the trail he had been following. Back he came to the big boulder. As before, he began sniffing around so much of it as did not lean against the precipice bottom.

"You fool!" rebuked Guy. "You've gotten off the track. You're following some ground-squirrel scent."

Dawn looked up, at his master's reproving tone. He eyed Manell in pained surprise. He returned to sniffing about the boulder's sides.

Dizzy, tired, nauseated, Guy slumped heavily against the boulder for support. Then he bounded back from it, as from a snake — fatigue and nausea forgotten.

The chest-high granite boulder — tons of solid weight — swung ponderously aside under his impact.

Slowly, heavily, noiselessly it swung, as might a huge metal door whose balance is true. For perhaps eighteen inches it swung, pivoting outward from the cliff-wall against which it rested. Then, as Guy sprang back, the release of his weight caused it to swing as slowly and as silently back into place.

Once more it was an ordinary boulder that had at one time tumbled to the mountain-foot and had found a resting-place amid fellow-rocks against the base.

For an instant as he blinked open-mouthed at the phenomenon, Guy thought he had overtaxed his injured head or else that Dr. Vreeland had been mistaken in saying the hurt was not serious. Rocks do not behave like that. Nor are sane people prone to "see things."

By an unbidden twist of memory, he was back in the assembly room of the Explorers Club, whither he had been taken as a guest by one of his instructors in the Columbia School of Mines. The speaker of the evening had been a savant who had spent years in the hinterland of Peru and of other South American countries with prehistoric pasts.

On the stereopticon screen had been flashed, successively, two pictures of the same gigantic rock: one as it reposed against a steep hillside; and one as it stood to one side, revealing a cave-mouth behind it. Manell could hear again the dry precise voice of the traveler explaining:

"The art of balancing and of pivot leverage was reduced to perfection by these aborigines — to an extent never equaled in modern times or with present-day appliances. This rock, gentlemen, is estimated to weigh four-and-a-quarter tons. Yet so delicately is it adjusted on a set of graduated under-stones that a single strong push is sufficient to move it to one side on its pivot, giving access to the subterranean temple's entrance, as you see.

"A somewhat similar principle was employed, on a smaller scale, by the ancients, in Egypt and in Palestine and elsewhere, to secure the entrance of tombs against wild beasts. Specially balanced stones or slabs of rock were used as doors for such tombs. By a process of leverage, they could be rolled away with comparative ease. You will recall also the fabled rock that masked Ali Baba's treasure cave."

Manell felt the nameless thrill of discovery. Here, in southern California, apparently, was just such a rolling stone as the explorer had described — here in this scene of another prehistoric civilization.

Cautiously he touched the boulder. Trying to find again the precise spot at which he had been standing and to duplicate the same direction of leverage, he pushed. It stood firm.

Thrice, from different angles, he threw all his power into the push. Thrice, the rock remained immovable. The fourth time, he succeeded.

Shifting his position ever so little, he shoved again. Slowly the vast rock gave way, under the steady pressure. It moved as if with intelligent reluctance. But it moved.

Little by little, he increased the pressure. At last, the boulder came to a stop in its semicircular motion. Try as he would, Manell could thrust it no farther on its pivot.

He held one hand on it, bracing himself against its tendency to swing back into place. Then, through the fading light, he looked at the space it had been concealing.

The collie's sudden ferocious snarl was echoed by Manell's own gasp of wonder. The sunset light had crept higher and higher. Now it bathed in crimson the topmost peaks of the nearby mountains. It had risen three-fourths of the way to Grudge Mountain's summit. The deep gorge at the bottom was in steadily deeper dusk.

Yet there was enough light left for Guy Manell to see that the pivoting of the boulder revealed an opening in the cliff-foot, perhaps a yard in height and nearly as wide across.

Straight up from it, and just inside the aperture, arose a flight of hewn stone steps which vanished into the very heart of the mountain. Dim as was the daylight outside, Guy could see, by stooping down, that the steps led steadily upward, inside the cliff.

He could see also that, though incalculably old and worn down by innumerable footprints, they were not the rude-hacked notches that might have been expected as footholds for savages. These hewn stairs revealed careful and clever workmanship. They were broad and even and well-graded. Here had wrought skilled artisans

190

under the direction of a master of his craft.

Instinctively, Guy had caught hold of Gray Dawn's cuff, as the collie, with a snarl, had darted forward into the opening. Now, dragging back the growlingly eager dog, he bade him lie down. Dawn, still growling and with hackles bristling, obeyed. He had the air of a beast checked just as it has run a victim to earth.

"No doubt of it, old friend," whispered Guy, soothingly, "you've scented him here. But here you've got to drop the trail. Somehow or other he got inside the lower ledge, this morning, and then downstairs here with me and so out, through that gap. You've solved it. No use in your rushing up those steps in there and maybe getting thrown over the cliff for your trouble. Stay where you are."

Manell stood for a minute in excited thought. He was unarmed. He had no light. Feverishly anxious as he was to fathom the mystery whose clue he had come upon so strangely, yet he was not a born fool.

He knew he could find nothing, in the black darkness of the mountain's interior, without so much as a single match to guide his steps. He knew, too, that in the dark, lost and unarmed, he would be at a pitiful disadvantage against any possible dwellers of the place. The memory of the giant hand was strong upon him.

"There's only one thing we can do, Dawn," said he, as ever talking to his dog as to a fellow-human. "We've got to wait until we have flashlights and a gun. Then we can go ahead. Just now, it's our move to shut up this hole and to clear out of here before anyone finds out we've learned how to get in. If we can!"

Chapter 22

Tugging and guiding, Manell got the swaying stone back into place, until it stood as before, with no hint of what it concealed. Then, snapping his fingers to Dawn, he turned homeward through the dusk. A hundred yards farther on, Guy stopped and looked back at the looming bulk of grim mountainside that towered so grimly above him; its verdure-patched crest still flecked by sunset glow.

"H'm!" he informed Dawn. "See that mountain? Well, it's a monster beehive of life. At least, it must have been, once; and we know there's life left inside it, even now — some weird form of life with a murderous intelligence, Dawn. The whole mountain is full of rooms or cells or caves, connected with stairways and with hidden exits; and with openings made so cunningly that they don't show from below here. Openings that stones can be thrown from, Dawn; or that arms can reach out of, to cut ropes. That's what happened to the Mexican officer. It's — it's a big many-storied house or temple. And those two ledges are its balconies. Why, Dawn, it must have taken those old aborigines centuries of time and swads of skill and labor to turn the inside of a mountain-peak into an enormous house! Talk about your cliff-dwellers! They weren't a patch on the prehistoric race that did this."

The dog wagged his tail interestedly, whenever he heard his name mentioned. The rest of the oration was of course unintelligible to him. Ever he peered truculently at the trail behind him. Manell turned on his heel and set off afresh for Friendly Valley.

To his surprise, he was none the worse for his long walk. Indeed, since that brief spell of sick dizziness at the mountain-foot, he felt practically no ill-effects from his hurt. His head was still excruciatingly sore to the touch. But his strength and youth and resiliency were dissipating more and more of the nerve-shock which was the principal after-effect of his mishap.

He reached home in better condition than when he had left it.

"A good supper will put me a hundred per cent on my feet again," he told himself, as he neared the porch.

Klyda Graeme was standing on the steps, awaiting him. She was visibly anxious.

"Oh, *why* did you do it?" she demanded, a thread of irritation in her soft voice. "I was so worried! The doctor told you to stay still and —"

"And he said I'd be as good as new by to-morrow morning," he cut in. "Well, he got the date mixed. I feel as well as ever, right now. The day's loafing and the sleep and all your dandy nursing, have cured me in no time. I —"

"And that's all the good my nursing and my worry did!" she chided him. "As soon as my back was turned, you rambled off for an hour's walk. I never heard of such a babyish —"

"When I was a kid at Pompton," he interrupted, solemnly, "I fell into the Ramapo River. Then I hid in the woods till my clothes dried. A fellow had seen me going toward the water. He told my mother. When I didn't show up at dinnertime, she was crazily anxious about me."

"Why not? She —"

"She was sure I was drowned. While my father was diving into the creek to find my body, she kept saying I was the darlingest and loveliest child she ever had; and she kept talking about how much she adored me."

"That is a mother's nature, isn't it?" asked Klyda, her annoyance unabated.

"Well, then I came sneaking out of the woods. Do you know what was the very first thing she did, to show how unspeakably dear I was to her? She gave me a spanking that sounded like a whole audience applauding. She got as mad as wrath with me. Just because she had been so scared. . . . I wonder if all women are alike, that way, when they find they've been scared for nothing."

Without deigning a reply, Klyda went loftily into the house. Guy followed. But she was not lightly to be moved from her fit of pique. Indeed, it was not until after supper, as they sat on the veranda, that she unbent altogether. Then, gradually, her normal manner returned; and with it the odd tinge of deprecation or even of apology which Guy had noted and puzzled over, during the past two days.

They chatted on indifferent subjects, for a time, there in the cool starlit darkness. But ever they found themselves falling silent, for no cause; as is said to be the way of man and maid at a stage when mere acquaintanceship seeks to merge into something less impersonal.

Klyda seemed to realize this. For she broke one such pause by asking abruptly:

"Did you have a pleasant visit from your friend, Mr. Negley? And did the poor old gentleman still think he knew Dad fifty years ago?"

"No, to both questions," answered Guy. "The call wasn't pleasant, because it broke up in my hurting his feelings; though I didn't mean to. And he doesn't think, any longer, that he used to know your father. That was what got him huffy. He asked me your father's name. When I told him, he thought I was guying him about his slip of memory and he walked out on me."

"How queer!" she commented. "I'm sorry. I left you because I thought you and he would like to chat together. And as soon as my back was turned you got to quarreling. Shame!"

He laughed at the motherly tone of her mock reproof. But he replied:

"No, we didn't get to quarreling, quite as soon as all that. He spent a little time, first, telling me how foolish the old-timers were to suppose there was gold hidden in one of these mountains."

To save his soul, Manell could not keep out of

196

the desultory conversation the theme that was filling his mind. To his surprise, Klyda leaned forward, through the soft gloom, and asked with a tinge of breathless interest:

"He says it isn't true? Not any of it?"

"Yes," answered Guy. "He says it all started with an Indian's lie. He says there isn't a word of truth in it."

"There *is!*" she cried, impulsively. "It's all true! Every word of it. And *more!*"

She shrank back, at his amazed stare; and she seemed to repent her strange burst of excitement. Then, before Guy could find words to frame his astonishment, the girl braced herself as for some harsh ordeal. She hurried on, in that same odd vehemence:

"It *is* true. All of it. I told Dad, yesterday and again today, that we have no right to eat your bread and stay under your roof, while we're deceiving you this way. It has made me so ashamed! Dad doesn't agree with me. But I know I'm right. I've never deceived anyone before. (I don't *think* I ever have.) And I hate it! We've no right to deceive *you*, of all people; after what you are doing for us. Besides, there's enough of it to make a hundred people rich, and —"

"Enough of what?" he blithered, dumbfounded at her torrent of shaken words. "What is there 'enough' of to — ?"

"Gold!" she caught him up, speaking almost hysterically. "Gold. Grudge Mountain is full of it. Not ore. Mined and refined gold. Stored there for centuries and centuries. *Millions and millions of dollars worth of it!* That's why Dad and I came out here to California."

Long and blankly Guy Manell gazed at her earnest little face, dim-seen through the dusk. Then he said:

"This is the second time today I've thought the crack over my head had addled what few wits I've got. But now, I'm dead sure of it. 'That's why Dad and I came out here to California,' eh? Why, you and he came out here to raise grapes. You bought —"

"To raise grapes!" she repeated, in sudden irritation. "What do Dad and I know about grape-raising or about any other kind of practical farming? He's a lawyer. Except for puttering around our Berkshire farm in summer, for the fun of it, he doesn't know the very first thing about farming. Why, we've both been horribly afraid you'd ask us some question that would expose his ignorance. All he knows of grape-growing is what he and I have been able to pick up from the Department of Agriculture bulletins he sent for before we left home."

"But —"

"Don't you see?" she went on, tremulously. "If we had come out here as tourists or even to buy a California home, it would have made people suspect something when we spent days in exploring Grudge Mountain. Besides, we couldn't carry the gold back and forth, in so many trips, without being suspected. But if we bought a ranch in a lonely place — not too near to the mountain to rouse suspicion by having such rocky land that nothing would grow on it, and not too far from it to transport the gold easily to our own cache — well, we could be pretending to look for water, there, for irrigation; and nobody would think twice about it or pay any attention to us. At least, that is what Dad and I believed. So we took up that miserable hillside tract."

"I see," he said, dully. "I see. This explains a lot of things that have been puzzling me. But it doesn't explain —"

"About the gold? That's what's made me feel so ashamed of myself. Dad said it was nobody's business but our own. But you've done so much for us! And I —"

"Hold on, please," he intervened. "I'm still in a muddle about this whole thing. But I gather you feel you ought to tell me some secret — or something you imagine is true — just because I happen to have been lucky enough to do one or two trifling neighborly good turns to you and your father. If that's the way it is, please stop right there. You don't owe me anything at all. And if you did, I wouldn't let you tell me some secret that you'd rather guard — just because you think it's honester to tell it. Please get that clearly in your mind, Miss Graeme."

The girl drew a long breath.

"You are a good deal of a man, Mr. Manell," she exclaimed. "I don't think any woman could have said what you've just said. She'd have been too inquisitive to —"

"She couldn't be any more inquisitive than I am about it," he confessed, embarrassed. "Nor any more flabbergasted. Only, I don't want to learn something that's told me on the ground that a guest thinks she owes it to me to tell. I —"

"But I *want* to tell you!" she urged, plaintively. "Can't you see? Apart from the meanness of deceiving you as we've been doing, we're helpless now, without you. Dad can't move a step, for weeks. You've been warned to leave here. So have we. The people in the Mountain guess what Dad and I are here for. They think you are joining us in the hunt. That is why they have warned you. You said, yesterday, that you still have a week to turn around in. Unless —"

"I see," he made answer. "I get the idea. Fire away. Perhaps I can piece out a few things that may have stumped you. Tell me your part of it, first. Then I'll tell you mine. Together, the two halves may amount to something. Or they may not."

She hesitated, as though she were trying to marshal in due order the facts of the narrative. Then, speaking with some difficulty but presently carried away by her own interest in her story, she began:

"In the first place, it'll make it easier to understand if I tell you why old Mr. Negley thought he recognized Dad. I didn't know. But Dad explained it to me, afterward. Mr. Negley mistook Dad for my grandfather — Dad's father and namesake."

"But —"

"The only pictures I ever saw of Grandpapa showed him in a full beard and heavy mustache and with a bald forehead. But Dad says he's seen a yellowed tintype of him, taken in 1870, at San Francisco, with a smooth face and before he lost his hair. He says that photograph is the living image of Dad himself. He says a few people have such strength of character and of physique — 'prepotency' is the science name for it, he says — that some of their children and grandchildren look almost exactly like them. Grandpapa must have been such a man. For, at fifty, he looked almost exactly like Dad. Dad says Grandpapa's face was more rugged and heavier. But it was enough like, to bring back the vision of it to Mr. Negley and make him think he was seeing his long-dead chum."

"But how did your grandfather happen to — ?"

"He was a miner, out in California. He was one of a group of men who came down here from Calaveras, when —"

"When that Indian renegade told his lie about — about the — ?"

"It wasn't a lie. That's why Dad and I are here. Let me tell you the whole thing from the very beginning. I'll make it as short as I can."

Chapter 23

Again she paused. Then:

"The rest of the miners who stampeded here when they heard the Indian's story were content with the bare outlines of it. Grandpapa wasn't. He had been a doctor, before he came out to the gold-fields. He had studied law, besides, when he was a young man. He used to question the Indian when they were alone, on the trip down from Calaveras. And then here, until the Indian was killed. This is what he found out:

"Centuries and centuries ago, there was an almost-white race — he thought they were prehistoric colonists from Peru or perhaps only from Yucatan — who settled around here. Long before the times of the Mexicans or the Spaniards or even the Indians. They were highly civilized and they were ruled by a priesthood. Grudge Mountain was their temple and their citadel.

"For hundreds of years they worked to hollow it out and to perfect it. Not only as abode for their priesthood, but as a treasure house and a fort as well. For by that time the first marauding bands of Indians — or perhaps of some other colonists from Yucatan or South America — had begun to clash with them. They needed an impregnable fort. They made one. And in it they stored all the treasure that was mined in northern Mexico or Nevada or higher up in California, and brought here, in taxes or as tribute or as votive gifts to the temple.

"This kept on for ever so long. The hoard grew to be so immense they were afraid word of it would get to some other nation and cause a conquest-war. That was what they were most afraid of, because they had begun to dwindle and weaken. There were pestilences, I suppose, the way there were in other races that are extinct. And the Indians were always warring with them.

"At last, there were only a handful of the old race left. Then came a new raid of the Indians, from a tribe that the Shoshones are descended from. They had no idea about the treasure, and they wouldn't have known what to do with it if they had; for they were savages. Not even barbarians. (Dad says pottery-making was the first dividing line between savages and barbarians.) They wanted the land. And they took it.

"The few people who remained of the old race still had their hoard and their citadel and their priests. But that was all they had. They schemed how to keep all three. And they hit on a really clever plan. This is what they did:

"They cultivated the friendship of one or two of the head men among the Indians that had taken possession of the region. They got these interested in a secret cult they practiced. A form of Masonry, Dad says. They made it seem a high privilege for the Shoshones to belong to the secret order, and to intermarry with the few men and women left of the old inhabitants.

"In this way, they formed a sort of inner circle of Indian chiefs and of their own survivors and of the children of the intermarriages. These people became the keepers of the hoard and of the rest of the mountain's secrets. The tribe at large could only hear rumors of it all; and they weren't even allowed to set foot within the sacred mountain.

"This impressed them and it gave them all sorts of superstitious reverence for the inner clan of priests and guardians who ruled the mountain.

"In time, the last members of the old race died out, except as some of their blood was carried on through the inner circle of Shoshones their ancestors had initiated into the cult. But the cult itself kept on. It was passed along from generation to generation; just as it used to be in Egypt, you know. There was a distinct clan or aristocracy that continued to be guardians of the mountain and its secrets.

"By the middle of the nineteenth century, this clan had dwindled to one or two families. The rest of the Shoshones had stopped doing reverence to them or to the supposed Spirit of the Mountain. Most of them had even forgotten the whole cult. But this dwindling little group held onto its rites and its secrets, all the more closely and religiously, because the rest of their world had turned its back on the old worship.

"They kept their blood-lines distinct and they looked down on the common Indians. And their priesthood were chosen with as much care and ceremony as ever. They continued to guard the sacred treasure, even if they couldn't keep on adding to it. They were still the upholders of the ancient faith, even if there were no longer any outsiders to worship the mountain's Spirit or to reverence its priesthood or to regard the high-priest as a sort of god. It was rather pathetic, wasn't it?"

"In a way, I suppose. Yet —"

"Well, that is the story the renegade Indian told Grandpapa. This Indian was connected by blood with the priest clan, in some way. He used to brag to Grandpapa that he was above the common Shoshones who lived around here in those days. He had even been anxious to join the priesthood; and he had served in the temple, as a boy. Then, because he tried to steal some of the treasure and was caught, he was banished from the mountain and from this whole region.

"In revenge, and because he wanted to be rich, he told his story. He had wonderful faith in the power of white men to do anything. He inherited it from the reverence they all had, in the temple, for their old half-white ancestors. He thought Grandpapa and the rest could help him overthrow the handful of priests and get hold of the treasure. He told Grandpapa ever so much more about it than he told the others."

"But —"

"Grandpapa wasn't just a visionary adventurer, like the rest of his party. He had gone scientifically to work at mining, up above Calaveras. He hadn't made a million. But he had made a comfortable little fortune, for those days. He had it transferred to an eastern bank. And he was just about to start back to Boston, to take life easy for the rest of his days, when he heard this Grudge Mountain story. It took hold of his imagination. It became almost a mania with him. He said it seems to have that sort of magic effect on everyone who gets in touch with it. He decided to have a try at testing its truth, before he went home.

"Well, a Pomptonian among them bribed the Indian to go out to the mountain alone with him, to show him the way. That was the first morning the party got here and while the others were still making camp. A man named Zabriskie. Their bodies were found, next day. They had been killed by a landslide, while they were climbing."

"*Perhaps!*" put in Guy, recalling his own recent experience with that variety of "landslide."

She did not hear his interpolation.

"The rest of the party were all at sea, now that their Indian guide was dead. They kept up the hunt for a while, Grandpapa along with this Mr. Negley. Then all of them except Grandpapa decided the thing was a hoax; and they gave it up. He kept on. You see, from the things the Indian had told him, he had his own theories. He hadn't said anything about these theories to the others; and he had pretended to follow out their plans of finding the treasure. He wanted it all to himself, in case it should ever be found. I'm afraid Grandpapa wasn't very open-hearted or altruistic."

"Few of us are, on a treasure-hunt," commented Guy. "Whether it is in Wall Street or at Grudge Mountain."

"The Indian had told him about the steep groove cut in the mountainside, up to the second ledge," she continued. "It had been hewn, so the common people of the tribe could climb to the ledge for worship and for sacrifice. Nobody but the inner circle knew the secret of getting inside the mountain. But he made a guess at —"

"I wondered how any convulsion of nature could have cut the groove into that geometrical trough-shape," said Manell. "But what — ?"

"I'm coming to that. Grandpapa tried a new angle, for the treasure, as soon as he had the field to himself. He knew it was out of the question for him to get into the mountain and to get hold of all the treasure and then to get out with it, before the priests should catch him at it and kill him. So he took up a bit of government land, almost at the edge of the ravine. He pretended to start a cattle ranch there, on a small scale. That's where Dad got our own idea of —"

"I see," assented Manell. "Mighty smart."

"Grandpapa had a good deal of a way with him," said Klyda. "And he had lots of magnetism. People always were attracted to him. He set out to make the acquaintance of the Shoshone Indians around here, by doing favors for them. He had picked up bits of their dialect, while he was mining. And he had learned more of it from the renegade Indian.

"Little by little, he won their confidence. At last he became friendly with the priest family itself. He did that by setting the broken leg and collar-bone of a girl who had slipped and fallen from a cliff near Grudge Mountain. She was the daughter of the high-priest. I told you Grandpapa was a doctor, though he had never made a success either of that or of the law.

"Well, it seems barbarians and savages have an almost superstitious respect for doctors. When the girl's broken bones were set and she was cured, Grandpapa brought the high-priest himself through a bad attack of typhoid. That settled it. They made him one of themselves."

"Then — ?"

"Oh, of course they never let him into the mountain. The priest's family lived in an adobe house on a ridge across from it. But with the information the renegade had given him, Grandpapa was able to find out for himself who was who. There was only one priestly family left, at that time. The old high-priest and his middle-aged son and this young daughter. The high-priest told Grandpapa he was not an everyday Indian, but a lineal descendant of the white Incas of Peru.

"Then Grandpapa did a hideous thing. He did it to make them think he was one of them, so they would trust him and tell him the secret of the treasure and how to find it in that labyrinth inside of the mountain."

She paused. Manell asked, curiously:

"What was the 'hideous thing' he did? Murder the high-priest?"

"Worse. He married the high-priest's daughter."

"What was there so 'hideous' about that?"

"Why, don't you see: He didn't love her. He married her only for the sake of getting hold of the treasure. He thought they'd admit him to priestly rank and all that. He wasn't one bit in love with her. That seems to me worse than if he had murdered her father."

"Oh!"

"But that's all the good it did him," she resumed. "They welcomed him into the family and they were proud to have a white man marry her. But they kept the secret from him. They didn't even know he had a clue to it or that he'd ever heard of it. The daughter didn't know how to get to the treasure, either. Because women weren't allowed inside the mountain.

"Perhaps in time they might have initiated Grandpapa into the mysteries. But he was impatient. He was so disappointed when he found he had gotten nothing by marrying the poor girl that he made up his mind to start a search on his own account. He had been watching the priests. Now he watched closer than ever. He found a way of getting into the mountain from that upper ledge."

"Good for him!"

"It was not!" she contradicted. "Don't you see? They trusted him, and he had wormed his way into their confidence to steal their hoard. He deserved what he got."

"What did he get?"

"Nothing. About two months after his marriage, he picked a time when he thought the high-priest and his son were away; and he climbed up to the higher ledge and went in through a hidden entrance. He found a great room, like a temple, with a flight of stone stairs leading up from it into the very heart of the mountain. He started to climb these steps, when the high-priest and his son sprang on him from behind. They threw a lariat around him and swathed him tight in it. Then they held a conference, what to do with him.

"The son was for killing him. Their rules decreed death to all spies. But the old man wouldn't do that, because Grandpapa had married his daughter. They compromised at last by letting him go, if he would leave California at once and never come back, and never tell any one what he knew of the mountain's secret.

"They made him swear it on his own Bible. Grandpapa did it, to save his life. He saw there was no chance for him to get at the gold, now that they were on the lookout for him. And a hundred men couldn't have captured the place by storm. So he took the oath. Then he came back East, to enjoy the little fortune he had scraped together in the mines. The next year, he married Dad's mother. I suppose it was legal for him to marry her. The other marriage had just been an Indian ceremony of some kind. Anyhow, he *did* marry her; though he never told her about his Indian wife. About a year after that, Dad was born. Both Dad's parents died when he was a little boy."

"You say he never told his wife —"

"He never told anyone. He kept his oath. That seems to be about the only redeeming feature of his awful conduct."

"Then how on earth did you ever get hold of the story you've been telling me?"

"Last year, Dad and I were going over a lot of rubbish in the attic of our farm, near Pittsfield, where we spend our summers. Dad was born there; and Grandpapa died there. In the garret there were some trunks with things that had belonged to Grandpapa. One of them, the littlest, was cramfull of old letters and newspapers and all sorts of useless documents, that nobody had ever bothered to sort over, after he died. They weren't his legal papers, you know. I suppose the executors had just glanced at them and decided they were no use to anyone, and had left them there.

"While we were clearing out the trunk, I ran across a calfskin account book. In it, Grandpapa had written all this story. I suppose he did it, in odd times, to amuse himself. He said, at the beginning of the account, that he didn't consider that a breach of his oath, as he planned to burn the book before he died. He said he wanted to set down the whole thing, because it reminded him, in his placid later life, that once he had been on the verge of great wealth and power.

"I read it aloud to Dad. The more we talked it over, the more excited we got. At last, Dad decided to come out here and look for the treasure. More than half a century had passed since Grandpapa was here. There had been only three of the priest family left then. One of those was a very old man and one was a woman.

"The chances all were that the whole family had died out, in the past fifty years, and the secret with them. Their hoard was lying there, useless; and it belonged to anyone who could find it. Just as much as the ore in the mountains does. For that matter, as Grandpapa pointed out, in his account, it hadn't belonged to the priests, even in his time. It represented the pillage and the taxes and the temple offerings of a race that didn't exist any more. So we came here.

"But, the priest family *isn't* extinct. It is stronger and more venomous than ever. That's been proved, in the past few days. Besides, Dad and I went up the groove to the ledge. And we couldn't find any possible way to get into the mountain."

For a minute after she had ceased her recital, Guy Manell sat silent. Then, quietly, and as briefly as possible, he told her of his own discoveries.

She listened, breathless, her slender body tense and vibrant.

As he ended his narrative, she jumped to her feet with an electric eagerness that roused the sleeping collie at her side.

"We are going there!" she declared, aquiver with excitement. "We are going there. We are going to get it, you and I. It is as much ours as it is those Indians'. The whole secret is in our hands, now. We know the way into the mountain. All we need do is to keep on till we find the treasure chamber."

" 'We'?" he repeated, no shade less thrilled than she. "It is no job for a woman. It may mean death. I am going there. I had made up my mind to it, before you told me all this. I'll share, equally, with you people, of course, in all I find. But I won't let you risk your life in —"

"You'll let me go with you!" she insisted. "If you won't, I shall go alone. Dad can't go, for weeks, yet. And we haven't weeks to wait. In less than one week the time given you in that last warning will be up. *We* are going. You and I."

Infected by her mad zest, he gripped the little hand she held out to him.

"You and I!" he echoed, wondering at his own acquiescence in so insane a scheme, yet realizing she would make good her threat to go alone, if he should refuse. "When shall we start? Now?"

"No. Wait. Let me think."

In a moment, she said:

"I have it. The priests, or whoever they are, have given you a week to leave here. They will be on the lookout, or have some spy on the lookout, to see whether or not you show any sign of obeying that warning. Good! Tomorrow morning, tell your foreman you have to go East, at the end of this week, and that you may not be back for a long time. Hint to him that you may not be back at all. Seem confused and frightened when you talk to him. Tell Sing, too. Drive over to Santa Dereta in the morning and say the same thing there; and make arrangements to have your luggage shipped to the station."

"But why?"

"Then come back here and haul all your trunks out on the veranda and begin packing some of them. Tell Sing and the foreman that Dad and I are going back East with you."

"Again, why?"

"The news will be all over the ranch and all over the neighborhood, by afternoon. From the top of Grudge Mountain, this veranda can be seen. Let it be seen with trunks and clothes littering it."

"You mean — ?"

"I mean they'll think they've scared you off, at last. That will make them sure they've nothing to fear from you and that they needn't be on guard."

"Splendid!"

"Then, tomorrow night, late, we'll go there," she announced.

"Tomorrow night!"

Again their hands met, clasping tight in a grip of compact.

The die was cast. The next twenty-four hours were to decide whether fortune or death should await them in the sinister recesses of the sacred mountain.

"By the way," asked Guy, as an afterthought. "I — I suppose your grandfather didn't say anything about — about anything as impossible and — and as absurd as a — a Giant fifteen or twenty feet high, guarding the treasure, did he? Because, unless I was dreaming, that day on the upper ledge, I caught hold of his hand. Best change your mind and let me go there alone."

Even as he spoke, he knew she would not consent.

Before she could answer, something smote resoundingly upon the adobe floor between them. At the impact, they started in alarm. The collie once more jumped up, barking angrily.

"Quiet, Gray Dawn!" commanded Guy, striking a match to investigate the nature of the flung object.

On the floor, at his feet, lay a white lump. He picked it up. It was a page of ordinary writing paper, tied with twine about a fragment of stone.

Without a word, man and maid hurried indoors, to the hall-lamp; while Dawn sniffed in vain for a clue to the stone-thrower. The evening wind blew smartly athwart the veranda, from end to end, baffling his attempt.

Under the lamp, Guy loosed the bit of twine and unfolded the paper. In a neat hand and in ink was written:

"Don't wait out the week. Go not later than the day after tomorrow. This at any sacrifice. If you will consent, tie a sheet to a branch of the orange tree in your dooryard. If not, may your God help you, for I cannot!"

"Where are you going?" asked Klyda, as Guy started down the hallway.

"To get a sheet," he called back to her. "It's got to be tried tomorrow night, now, whether we want it to be or not. It's our last chance."

Chapter 24

On the stroke of midnight, next evening, Guy and Klyda crept guiltily from the cottage, with the air of stage burglars.

Each carried two flashlights, and spare batteries. In Guy's belt was his service pistol, newly oiled and reloaded. In the breast of Klyda's outing-shirt snuggled the ridiculous little automatic pistol wherewith she had once threatened Manell.

They had left Gray Dawn indoors. On such a venture the collie was not likely to be of any use whatever; and his habit of breaking into explosive fanfares of barking in any moment of excitement was by itself enough to bar him from this stealthy expedition.

He had run expectantly to the front door, as they started forth, only to find the door shut in his chagrined face, with scant ceremony.

Wordless, with every faculty keyed high, the two passed out of the sweet seclusion of Friendly Valley. They made their way along the broken trail toward Grudge Mountain. The night was still and overcast. There was a breathlessness to the air, unusual in that breeze-swept region.

All day had the knotted sheet dangled ostentatiously from the dooryard orange tree. All day had the cottage-veranda been cluttered with trunks and clothing. All day had Guy been making fussy arrangements for departure.

He and Klyda had decided to say nothing to Saul Graeme about their plan for the night. All the slowly-convalescing oldster knew was that there was talk of moving away. To tell him of their purpose and then to leave him worrying in impotent solitude while they were absent, seemed needless cruelty.

"In your grandfather's time," said Guy, as he and Klyda neared the mountain, "you told me the high-priest and his family didn't actually live in the mountain, but in an adobe house across the gorge. Probably it's the same, now, when there is no reason for standing guard. They'll have seen the sheet we tied to the orange tree; and they'll have heard we're getting out. That means they'll be in their own house and not in the mountain. Let's hope so, anyhow."

Klyda made no reply. Her whole mind and soul were set upon the adventure ahead of them, as she moved forward, wordless and rapt. Guy did not speak again as they stole on. But for the occasional click of a pebble or the snap of a dry twig under their moccasined feet, the night silence was unbroken by their tread. They moved steadily, but not fast. For the darkness made rapid walking hazardous; and they dared not flash their lights.

After an eternity, Guy stopped alongside the rock whose secret of locomotion he had mastered on his twilight visit, two days before. Again he tested it from various points, before he happened on the one direction from which, and in which, it could be moved.

Soundlessly, the big boulder swung sideways under his pressure. As it reached its farthest arc, he whispered to Klyda. The girl took from under his arm the two light crowbars he had brought along for the purpose. These she propped against the rock, close together, striking their sharpened points into the earth and fixing the other ends beneath inequalities of the boulder's side.

Her task done, Guy released his own weight from holding back the rock. It settled against the propping crowbars and held there.

Against the dim gray of the mountain-base, the aperture behind the boulder showed like a patch of slightly denser darkness. Guy knelt, and crept in on all fours, leading the way. Klyda followed.

The man went first, because of his memory of the rattle-snake whirr that sounded as he had entered the opening in the upper ledge. But he had lived long enough in the wilds to know that snakes are seldom abroad at night and that there was no great danger of encountering one at this hour.

His outstretched hand touched one of the lowest of the hewn rock-stairs. In another moment he and Klyda were ascending the flight.

In the pitchy darkness the man collided with a wall, at his sixth step. He paused and felt his way.

By touch he realized he had come to a turn or an angle in the flight, and had walked straight against the rock.

"This won't do," he whispered. "There may be jumping-off places or wells in the stairway or chasms at either side. I'll have to turn on the light. No one could see it from outside, now that we've gotten as high as this, and turned the corner."

He took out one of his two strong flashlights and pressed its button. The flood of radiance revealed them standing on a small stone landing, at the top of the first few stairs of the flight. Thence, at a right angle, the steps continued directly upward, farther than the flashlight's ray could penetrate with any clearness.

The stairway was perhaps six feet in width. The age-worn steps were low and broad and of perfect evenness. On either side the rough-hewn walls rose to a still rougher stone roofing, some eight feet above the steps. The explorers were in an upward-slanting tunnel, about eight by six feet in area.

"Funny!" mused Guy as they continued their climb, turning the flashlight on, for an instant, at every ten or fifteen steps. "The air in here is clean and breathable. Not even a musty smell to it, the way there is in mine-shafts. I don't understand."

"I do," she answered in the same guarded tone. "I saw, just now, when you turned the light on. Do it again."

He pressed the flash-button.

"Look," she said, pointing ahead and to one side.

Some twenty feet beyond was another rude landing, whence the stairs took a new angle. The left wall of this angle was pierced by a loophole window, cut in the rock, on much the principle of the arrow-loopholes in a mediaeval castle.

On the floor of the landing, directly beneath the window, a small heap of stones was piled.

"For air and for light and for observation and for stone-dropping," said Guy, staring at the window. "The chaps who did this were crafty artisans. They've taken advantage of some irregularity in the outer wall of the cliff, so the loophole isn't visible from the ground below. Probably there are a hundred such loopholes, scattered here and there, from top to bottom of the mountain — all invisible from outside. No wonder they can aim rocks down at intruders, so well! I suppose the stone heaps were put here, ages ago, for use in case of a siege. Let's go on."

They put out the light and made their way upward, along an interminable number of steps. At length one of the occasional flashes of Guy's electric torch revealed the end of the curving flight.

Presently they reached another and far larger landing; in fact it was a small gallery room from which tunnels wound into the rock at either side. Here were no piercing windows through the face of the outer wall. In their stead a square-cut hole in the wall was stopped from the far side by the bulging surface of such a boulder as marked the entrance at the mountain-foot.

Guy studied the big stone, for a moment. Then he said:

"I know where we are, and why there aren't any loopholes here. This must be the rolling stone that they push aside to get out onto the lower ledge. It must be in through here that Tawakwina carried me, after one of his priest friends had bowled me over with that stone. Whew! I don't envy him the job of toting me all the way down those stairs on the way out. I wonder why they let him do it. If they wanted to kill me, enough to drop stones on me, why didn't they finish the job while I was at their mercy?"

To the left of the rolling stone, and alongside one of the two branching tunnels, the stairway recommenced. The adventurers continued their silent climb. Their ascent was broken, here and there, as before, by small landings, pierced with loopholes. Always under each loophole were stones of varying sizes.

"It was from one of these they watched me," said Guy. "And when they got me in range, they began stoning me."

The stair grew steeper. Both climbers were breathing hard when an abrupt turn in the flight brought them to a second and far larger gallery. Guy was leading the way. His flashlight's gleam fell on a tangle of vines, across an opening in the wall.

"Hello!" he whispered back to Klyda. "This must be the higher ledge. There's the vine screen

I crawled through. The same hole your grandfather came through, when they nabbed him. And I believe I know why the vines are there, instead of a rolling stone. The stone must have gotten displaced in some earthquake; and the Shoshones didn't know the art of putting it back on its pivots so as to make it work. You know it was the old race and not the Shoshones who made this place. The Indians weren't able to put it back, in a way that would let them out and in. So they trained that clump of bushes across the opening, to hide it. They —"

He started violently. The flashlight, straying from the aperture, had fallen first on a continuation of the upward-leading flight of steps. Then it had played across the deep gallery. Now, almost directly in front of the screened opening, it came to rest upon a truly astounding object.

There, looming high above them was a human figure, carved out of jet black rock — a statue whose damp stone surfaces glistened in the white light. It was the figure of a gigantic man with noble and austere countenance. One hand held a serpent-headed scepter. The other hand was outstretched.

Guy Manell drew a long breath of relief. His one fear in the venture — the nameless terror of the supernatural — fell away from him. Here then was the gigantic ice-cold hand with which his groping fingers had come in contact that day when he crept through the screen of vines into this pitch-dark place. He could have laughed aloud, from sheer reaction.

Henceforth, this promised to be a delightful tour of exploration. At worst, mere humans like himself were to be arrayed against him. Not impossible giants with icy hands thrice the size of his own. He found himself gazing with a certain friendliness at the bugaboo statue.

No Indian, assuredly, had designed or carved that supremely artistic form. It was worthy the chisel of a Canova. Half-nude, half-clad in a flowing robe of stone feathers — and Guy recalled reading that feather robes among the Incas served the same sumptuary purpose as robes of ermine in mediaeval royalty — the giant was crowned with something not unlike the Triple Uraeus Crown of the Pharaohs.

Here apparently was the statue of some early priest-king of that extinct race, perpetuated forever in onyx, in the halls that he or his ancestors had carved from the solid rock.

Beside him was a square block of fire-stained white marble, a trough fluting its outer edges.

"Their ancient altar!" whispered Guy. "See the places for the blood of the burnt offerings to run off into that hole in the floor. Human sacrifices, most likely, to judge from the rites of the Aztecs and the Peruvians."

But for the statue and the altar the great vaulted gallery was bare. As Guy and the girl turned toward the ascending stair, a faint hiss sounded behind them, followed by a drowsy whirring. Manell flashed the light in the direction of the sound.

Up from the hollowed space beneath the altar a rattlesnake was rearing its ugly arrow-shaped head. Disturbed in its slumbers by steps and voices, the reptile looked forth malevolently at the intruders.

"He won't follow us," said Guy, reassuringly. "Rattlers never do. I suppose this place is swarming with them. Rattlers love rocky hillsides and sunny ledges, and dark lairs where they can hide. But they're decent enough to give warning. Don't be frightened."

"I'm not!" she whispered back, steadily. "Can't we go a little faster?"

"No," he answered. "We can't. This climb may last another half-hour. I'm not going to have you all worn out when we get to the treasure chamber — if there is one. Take your time. Keep your shoulders back and your lips closed and your elbows a little behind you. That's the way to climb long stairs without getting out of breath."

The next hundred yards were a repetition of the first. Interminable stairs, irregularly broken by landings, each with its loophole and its pile of stones. Here and there, at such landings, tunnels branched off, laterally.

Guy interrupted their climb by exploring two of these tunnels. He found they merely extended in a curve for perhaps three hundred feet in each direction, with loopholes and stone piles at intervals, terminating at last in the rock wall. As he and Klyda resumed their climb, after the second of these digressions, Guy said:

"That means they could command the valley and the gorge for a space of almost a furlong; and they had a battle-front of all that distance, besides getting a view in three directions. Their precious descendants could see the sheet on my orange tree from here, without any trouble at all. . . . I only hope they go on the principle of believing all they see."

"I've been thinking!" spoke up Klyda, presently, as they continued to mount. "You told me you found the groove all choked with rocks, and that some of the boulders on the upper ledge, that couldn't possibly have been swept down by the rest, were gone, too. I believe the old Inca race arranged all those rocks on their principles of leverage, so that they could be sent rolling down into the groove in case the mountain was attacked. Probably they had some simple system of mechanics for doing it. The secret passed on, through the ages, along with the other secrets of the mountain. And, the other day, the people who are here now put those principles into action, and stopped up the groove, so that you couldn't get to the ledge again."

Guy remembered the face he had half seen in the chaparral on the opposite hill, before he went into the cave. But once more the girl was speaking.

"Today," she said, "I ran across one of those books on Peruvian and Yucatan exploration, in your library. It didn't look as if it had ever been

226

read. Most of its leaves weren't even cut. I read a good deal of it — two or three chapters. And one of them started me thinking. I've an idea about those golden bullets. It just flashed into my mind. The book said that the high-priests — it was either in Yucatan or Peru, I'm not sure which — used no utensils or weapons that were not of solid gold. It was part of their religion. That clause in their creed may still obtain here. If it does — well, I suppose a solid gold gun is out of the question. But a solid gold bullet isn't. Besides, bullets of precious metal, with sacred charms muttered over them, have been supposed to have magical powers, in all primitive faiths. Don't you remember the silver bullet in *Der Freischutz* — and again in *Emperor Jones*? I believe it was the same principle that made them shoot at us with golden bullets. They —"

Again, she stopped short in her low-pitched speech. A pressure of the electric torch showed them a break in the stair; and beyond it was a vast space to either side — a space whose stone roof was ceiled with rotting planks.

Hastily, the two scrambled up what was left of the flight, wholly forgetting Guy's admonition to walk slowly and with closed lips and squared-back shoulders. In another ten seconds they found themselves in a great low-ceiled hall, several times larger than that of the temple below them. From here, no further ascending stairs were visible. Apparently, they had come to the summit of the edifice within the mountain.

Chapter 25

They paused at the top of the flight. Both of them were flashing their powerful torches on the strange scene about them. The first gleam had shown the center of the vast room to be empty.

For perhaps a hundred by a hundred feet the chamber stretched out, its massive lines marred by that absurdly low and broad-ceiled roof, scarce twelve feet high.

Against the walls and out halfway to the center of the room, were piled in mathematical neatness hundreds upon hundreds of bulging goatskin bags. They arose almost to the boarded ceiling in many places. Each was perhaps the size of a sack of meal. Each was tight-fastened at the mouth by wire cord.

Bags — *bags* — BAGS! In solid ranks they were stacked, well-nigh filling that area of a hundred by a hundred by twelve feet. There was a space, scarce twenty feet in every direction, cleared away at the head of the stairway; but all the rest of the enormous room was chokingly full of the fatly bulging goatskin sacks.

Girl and man stared in wide-eyed awe at the spectacle. Guy's throat was sanded. His eyes were blurred by the terrific force of the emotion that set his heart to thudding. He was carried out of himself by what he saw and by the tremendous significance of it all.

"The treasure-chamber!" he croaked, drunkenly. "Lord! Hundreds of tons of treasure! The accumulation of perhaps a thousand years! No wonder they can afford to mold their bullets out of pure gold! There must be more gold in this place than in all the mints in America and the Sub-Treasury, besides."

His own babbling voice came back to him in the echoes of the treasure-vault. Drunk as he was with the incredible wonder of it all, the blithering sound made him ashamed, and it sobered him. He glanced apologetically at Klyda.

She was staring tremblingly at the mountains of tight-packed bags. But there was no foolish exultation in her flushed face. Instead, Guy read there a real terror.

"I'm — I'm frightened!" she panted. "I promised you I wouldn't be. But I am. There's something so — so awful in the sight of all this. It's — why, it's the wealth of a whole continent. Think what it means! Oh, who are *we*, to touch it? Let's go back. I'm afraid of it."

"Nonsense!" he laughed reassuringly. "We haven't come all this way, just to turn and run because we have our fingers on more wealth than the Rockefellers ever dreamed of. It's ours. We settled all that. It doesn't belong to these Indians. It never did. It was collected for hundreds of years by a race that's extinct. It's nobody's. It's anybody's. It's — Lord, it's *OURS!!!*"

With braggart swagger he strode across to the nearest wall of sacks. Opening his jackknife, he drew the keen-edged blade down the burstingly full bag, from top to bottom.

"Let's have a look at some of our own fortune!" he exclaimed. "Turn your light full on it, so we —"

His words ended in a gurgle, as though strong fingers had gripped his windpipe. His jaw fell slack. His eyes bulged stupidly.

Under the dual glare of the flashlights the slit bag was disgorging its contents in a cascading torrent to the stone floor.

But that tumbling torrent did not give back the flashlight-radiance in the expected flame of golden beauty. Instead, a muddy, blackish-brown mass was pouring forward in sullen heaviness.

The despoiled bag collapsed limply to the floor and lay in a bunch atop its former contents. Guy stepped forward and picked up a handful of the stuff his knifeblade had let out of its age-old prison. At the first touch his hope died.

What he picked up had little weight to it and less of the gratifying hardness he had expected. He played his light on it, squinting closely down at the handful. Then he lifted it to his nostrils. Klyda's voice broke the stillness.

"I — I suppose it has tarnished, after all these centuries," she said, timidly.

She, too, had known shock, at the failure of their treasure to scintillate and glitter in the light.

"Yes," Guy made answer, his heart dead within him. "Yes, it has tarnished. It's done more than that. It's rotted."

As he spoke, he tossed the brown stuff contemptuously back into the heap, and glowered broodingly down upon it.

"I — I don't understand," faltered Klyda, taking a hesitant step forward and picking up a pinch of the bag's former contents. "I —"

With a spark of vague hope smouldering again in his breast, Manell went up to three other bags, at different edges of the cleared area. He treated each as he had treated the first, slitting it from top to bottom in a single sweep of his knifeblade.

From all of them cascaded that same blackish brown mass, slithering almost noiselessly to the stone floor.

"It's — What *is* it?" asked Klyda, piteous in her bewilderment. "It doesn't look or feel like any gold I ever —"

"Listen," said Guy, touched by her consternation and lifted by it out of his own selfish misery. "Listen, dear! Don't you know what this is? Why, it's corn!"

"Corn? But —"

"At least, it was corn, when it was stored here. It isn't much of anything, now. And it hasn't been, for hundreds of years. It isn't even as well-preserved as that sample of Egyptian wheat at Washington — the wheat they took out of the tomb of a Pharaoh. It's blighted, withered, rotted corn. It's the mouldy skeleton of corn. It

231

wouldn't grow, and it wouldn't be fit to eat."

"I — I can't understand!" she repeated, dazedly. "I can't understand, at all. They wouldn't have guarded decayed corn all this time. They wouldn't have killed people who tried to get to it. And besides, the golden bullets —"

"I don't know how to explain the golden bullets," he answered. "Probably they were melted down from some temple ornament that was left over. But I can explain this corn. So can you, if you'll stop to think for a moment."

"I —"

"In ancient days, corn was currency. So were oil and wine. We read that in the Old Testament. Especially among primitive people, like the race that built this room. Corn was their wealth — their medium of exchange. In good corn years they were rich. In lean corn years they either went broke or else had to draw on the corn they had stored from the fat years. Tribute and taxes were paid in corn."

"Then — ?"

"The race with the largest hoard of corn was the richest race. It was their Treasure. The treasure-yarn was handed down from generation to generation here, till it got to that renegade Indian and the rest. Of course they would have thought the only treasure in the world was gold. So they believed this was a storehouse of gold. That's the whole mystery cleared up. The priests guard this place from religious zeal. As Christians might guard a threatened church. Not to

232

protect its treasure. They know, as well as we do, that the treasure is rotted corn and that it isn't worth a penny, the whole lot of it. All they are doing is trying to keep outsiders from profaning their holy shrine. The corn is just a symbol."

For an instant, she looked at him as though she could not grasp his simple explanation. Then, to his dismay, she burst into a passion of tears. Sinking down amid the piles of decayed grain, she buried her face in her hands and swayed back and forth, her light body racked with sobs.

"Don't!" he besought, stricken by her uncontrollable grief. "Oh, *please* don't! I know what a smash this is to you, after you'd planned and dreamed of a fortune. But —"

"Fortune!" she echoed, sobbing. "It isn't that! The fortune is the littlest part of it. But to think that Dad was nearly killed — that *you* were nearly killed — that Dad is still in bed and suffering so — that our beautiful horses were killed and that your home must be given up — all for — for decayed *corn!*"

She broke into uncontrolled laughter, tears and hysterics warring with each other for mastery. Then — he never could explain how it happened — Guy Manell found himself sweeping the pathetic little figure up off the ground and clasping it tight to his breast.

"*I've* discovered treasure here, anyway!" he cried, seeking to kiss the wet face so close to his own. "Even if you haven't. Oh, girl of mine — let me keep the treasure that God has led me to!"

For an instant she struggled faintly. Then, inch by inch, her arms crept up, around his neck. As simply as two little children, man and maid kissed each other on the lips.

Then, from beneath their feet issued a right hideous clangor — a din that reverberated deafeningly throughout the dark spaces around them. It was as though a furious Giant were bellowing — a Giant incredibly huge and stertorous. The girl started nervously; but she clung the closer to her lover.

"What — what was that?" she whispered, in quick alarm.

"I don't know," he replied, deliriously. "Perhaps just an earthquake or a landslide or a band of avenging Indians or something. What does it matter? We're here, together. For always, *together!*"

Chapter 26

But he had no means of knowing whether or not she made answer. For, at that moment neither of them could have heard a trumpet call.

The clangor of that unearthly sound was swelling in volume. The mountain cavern rocked, and roared, with it. The myriad echoes caught it up and sent it banging from wall to wall and from landing to landing, until the frightful tumult hammered into the eardrums of man and maid like the outburst of a menagerie-ful of mad lions.

Guy had placed two of the flashlights in niches between bags, buttons still pressed forward, while he had examined the contents of the last two sacks. Now, he released the girl, and faced toward the stairway at his feet — the stairway whereby they had mounted to the treasure-chamber.

Up through this aperture was gushing that indescribable reverberating roar. Even it was growing more deafeningly loud, more unbearable to hear.

"What is it?" Klyda demanded once more, in a momentary lessening of the roll of din.

"Heaven knows!" he shouted back. "I know it isn't made by any human voice or by any instru-

ment. The thing is *alive,* that's making the un-
godly noise. But it isn't a human voice. Besides,
all the echoes and reverberations of those passages and stairways are magnifying it a hundred
times over. It —"

"There are people coming up here!" she cried,
breaking in on his perplexed homily. "Listen!"

And now, through the roaring clangor both
could hear the pad of human feet — feet that
were bounding up the long stair-flights, through
the darkness, with a speed and sureness that
spoke of long familiarity with the place. The fast-
onrushing footsteps sounded nearer than did the
approaching source of those detonating roars.

"They've found we're here!" exclaimed
Manell, after a second of listening. "And they're
rushing us. I can't tell how many there are. The
echoes make it seem like an army."

As he spoke he picked her up and thrust her
into the niche left by the emptying of two of the
sacks. Thrusting other bags out of the way, he
made a space for her, amid this corn barricade.
The flashlight-glare did not reach her in those
shadows.

"Stay there!" he commanded. "Don't move,
whatever happens. I need all my attention for
this job."

He drew his pistol and took up his place at the
narrow stair-head.

"They can't rush me, more than two abreast,
here!" he muttered, the zest of battle beginning
to burn in his heart. "Now then!"

Up out of the tunnel-like wall of the stairway sprang a naked man — a full-blooded Indian. He carried in one hand a rifle. The man was a Shoshone, though of coarser type than Tawakwina.

As he came into view within a few steps of the top, he whipped the rifle to his shoulder and fired pointblank at Guy Manell.

Guy had covered him with his pistol; and now, with steady nerve, he pressed the trigger.

The two reports sounded a fraction of a second apart, the rifle-shot belching forth first. The place re-echoed and thundered to the volley.

Guy reeled backward, the pistol flying from his grasp as though it were struck away by a giant hand. Its bullet tore through one of the grain-bags, letting out a dribble of rotted corn through the circular rent.

Manell staggered under an impact whose nature he could not guess. His right arm was numb to the shoulder, though he felt no pain. The Shoshone's rifle bullet had struck the barrel of Guy's outthrust pistol, glancingly, yet with such force as to rip the weapon out of its holder's hand and to benumb the whole arm.

The Indian did not pause to reload his old-fashioned single-shot rifle, but whirled it aloft, club-fashion. Clearing the topmost step, he hurled himself at the staggering Manell.

Behind him on the stairway appeared a second man. He carried a heavy-calibre old-style rifle; and he was following close behind the Shoshone.

Guy had no time nor scope to observe this newcomer. For the Indian was upon him. His right arm still numb and all but useless, Manell sprang back from the swing of the clubbed rifle.

Klyda Graeme sped forward from her alcove, leveling her tiny automatic at the charging Indian.

The Shoshone saw her. He flinched, for an instant, from the leveled weapon and the steady dark eyes behind it. This infinitesimal breathing-space gave Manell time to dodge back from the swinging rifle-butt, which missed his head by a bare inch.

Before the Indian could whirl the cumbrous weapon aloft again, Klyda pulled trigger.

There was a puny click. The hammer fell dully upon a defective cartridge. (Somewhere in an ammunition factory, far back in the East, a girl had stopped to gossip with a fellow-worker or had unfolded a new stick of chewing gum at the wrong time. Or a grimy man in a fulminate house had scamped his job in order to go home early to rest after a spree. As a result, a cartridge on whose perfection hung a human life, failed to explode.)

The Shoshone was quick to take advantage of the failure. Once again, with clubbed rifle, he charged upon the unarmed Manell. The man behind him, at the stair-head, had his own rifle at the shoulder. But he could not shoot, for fear of hitting his comrade, whose body was between him and the others.

Though all had been too engrossed to notice it, the reverberantly deafening clangor from below had increased momentarily in volume. Now, it resolved itself all at once into a sound familiar to everyone, though still magnified and distorted by the myriad uncanny echoes of the rock passages.

As the Shoshone sprang, something flashed past the other man at the stair-head — something silvery-gray and huge. A new and terrible factor had been added to the conflict.

Chapter 27

Sing had been awakened soon after midnight by the whining and scratching of the imprisoned collie. Thinking the dog had been left indoors by mistake and that his efforts to get free would keep the whole household awake, the Chinese cook had pattered grumblingly downstairs and had let him out. Instantly, Gray Dawn had found his master's trail and had followed.

Reaching the aperture at the base of the mountain, he had run in, and had pursued the scent upward, along the countless stairs. But at almost the first step he had caught a scent fresher than Guy's — the hated smell of an Indian. In blazing wrath, Gray Dawn had given tongue in a succession of furious barks which the echoes had changed into a plangent roar. Hot on the trail the big dog had galloped up the rock-hewn stairs.

Now, arriving just in time — not only to see the detested Indian, but to see that same Indian attacking the master he idolized, Gray Dawn went into whizzing action.

As the Shoshone leaped for Guy, the silver-gray catapult whizzed forward, through mid-air, straight and deadly as a flung spear. The collie crashed against the Indian's naked shoulders, from behind. His curved white eyeteeth raked the base of the man's skull.

Down to the rock-floor, under that seventy-pound weight, crashed the Shoshone, the rifle clattering to the floor, out of his reach. The great dog ravened upon him, like a wild beast worrying its prey. Dawn was seeking madly to get to the jugular. He ripped and tore at the frantic hands wherewith the Indian strove to fend him off.

Over and over rolled Shoshone and dog; while the whining snarls of the collie and the panic-screeches of his victim turned the re-echoing place into a bedlam of awesome din.

The man at the stair-head leveled his rifle again. But once more he could not shoot, lest his bullet miss the collie, in that whirling welter of fur and bare flesh, and kill his own companion.

Yet, now that dog and Indian were down, the space between Guy Manell and the newcomer was momentarily open. Guy could get a clear view of this second foe. At the sight, his brain became well-nigh as numb as was his arm.

For, at a glance, the man was Saul Graeme.

There were the same leonine head; the same rugged features; the same lowering expression. The resemblance, for an instant, was striking.

Then, almost at once, Guy saw this was not Klyda's father; even as his logic had told him it could not be. The face was leaner, and was higher of cheekbone and more aquiline of nose. The hair, too, was coarse and straight and jet black, not grizzled and curling. The skin was darker and had a coppery tinge. This was neither white man nor Indian, but a half-breed.

All these things he noted, subconsciously, and in a flash of time. So did Klyda who had cried out in consternation at sight of the man.

There was scope for no longer observation. For, turning from the two wallowing and rackety combatants on the floor, the newcomer stepped forward, rifle steady, and with deliberate aim covered Manell. His heavy face was expressionless, now, and it held the cold deadliness of a striking rattlesnake. Klyda cried out again. The half-breed's reptilian eye shifted to her for the merest fraction of a second. But again the lightning-brief diversion served.

At a bound, Guy Manell cleared the short distance between the half-breed and himself. Memories of football days made him tackle low.

Had he sprung at his foe at full height, a bullet must have stopped him, midway. But — as ever with those who are not expecting it — the whirlwind low tackle confused the half-breed. As he shifted his aim to cover the flying body, Guy caught him around the loins.

Back against the grainsacks crashed the two, from the force of the impact. And this accident made it impossible for Manell to gain the needed leverage to fling the other backward over his head. For the half-breed was too close-jammed against the sacks to be lifted thus.

Instantly, Guy shifted his grip, seeking the

underhold, at the small of the back. But again he failed. He was encountering a man larger and more solidly muscular than himself — a man who, for all his bulk, was as quick of motion as a panther.

The half-breed twisted lithely to one side, at the same time shortening his grip on the rifle and turning its muzzle against Manell's breast. Guy released his futile grasp of the man and struck the muzzle upward with all his strength and speed. Barely was he in time. For, as he struck, the half-breed pulled trigger.

The bullet flew high. It plowed its ripping way through the rotten ceiling-planks just above the head of Klyda Graeme, as she crouched against the barrier of grainbags.

The half-breed did not hamper himself with a weapon that was of no further use to him. At such close quarters there was no hope to use it, clubwise, as had his companion. For Guy was grappling him afresh, striving as before for the fatal underhold.

The rifle was allowed to drop from the hand that could be better used without it. The half-breed wheeled with the tense fury of a wildcat upon his smaller opponent.

Guy's numb right arm had come to life again, with a million pringles of pain as circulation and strength returned to it. Yet he needed all his prowess and all his swiftness, to cope with this gigantic enemy whose attack was more that of a maddened beast than of a human.

The half-breed swung Guy clear of the floor and strove to heave him aloft to dash him to the rocks or down the steep stair-well. Guy writhed, snakelike, in the mighty arms, twisting his shoulder against the giant chest, and driving the heel of his left hand upward with all his might against the granite chin of his adversary.

The jarring impact of this street-fight manoeuvre loosened the constrictor arms, for the moment, ever so slightly. Before the grip could tighten again, Guy had wriggled eel-like out of their reach.

He saw he was no match for his Hercules foe, at close grips. And it dawned upon him that his best chance was at boxing. Presumably this Samson had no knowledge of the art. Most savages are ignorant of it. In any case, it seemed the one possible way to oppose him.

Wherefore, as the half-breed bore ferociously down upon Guy, he was met by a straight left-hander to the point of the jaw, from the man whom he had expected to grapple. The blow was well delivered by trained muscles and with a braced body behind it. As it smote upon his jaw-point, the giant swayed back on his heels, his mighty arms flying wide. Before he could re-cover, Guy was at him with a hurricane of short-arm smashes to heart and wind, and with all his weight behind each whalebone punch.

Under the crashing fusillade, the larger man was driven back against the wall of sacks, striking futile hammer-blows at his smaller antagonist —

blows as fearsome as they were awkward — blows which would have killed, if they had landed square.

But Guy never was there, when they were struck. With all his old-time boxing skill and gift for footwork, he blocked or ducked them, one after another, ever countering with some well-placed punch to a vital spot.

Driven against the bags the giant sought furiously to clinch. Guy slipped back from the grabbing arms. Then with the speed of light he darted in and landed a right swing to the battered jaw. The blow banged its recipient's head back against a sack with a piledriver force that burst the tough goatskin and sent the bag's rotting contents in a shower over both fighters.

Had the resilient bag been solid wall, the battle would have ended, then and there, with a knockout. But the half-breed, dizzy and almost stunned, merely bounced forward, from his own impetus — forward to meet a second homicidal right swing for the jaw.

Guy Manell threw every atom of his skilled strength and every ounce of his weight into this punch — a punch his foe was too dazed, for the instant, to guard or to draw back from. No professional pugilist could have received it full on the jaw-point and have kept his footing.

But, as he pressed his toes hard against the rock-floor, to add force to his swing, Guy's moccasined soles encountered a handful of the slimy rotted grain that had debouched from the burst sack. The effect was much the same as when the toe of a runner chances to land obliquely upon a banana-peel on a sidewalk.

Both feet went from under Manell. The terrific blow for the jaw fell scrapingly against the half-breed's chest, instead of reaching its vulnerable destination. Down went Guy, jarringly, on both knees.

The daze-mists clearing from his brain, the giant hurled himself upon his half-prostrate opponent. Guy scrambled up, by the time his knees had fairly touched ground. But the fragment of wasted time had changed the tide of the whole fight.

Before Guy was fairly on his feet again — before he could strike or so much as jump back out of the way or clinch — the half-breed seized him in his knotty arms and lifted him aloft. Then, as Manell writhed to get free or to strike at the face or body so jammingly close to his own, the giant pinioned him with one arm, and with the fingers of the free hand found Manell's throat.

Into Guy's mind swam the unbidden thought:

"My life — and if mine, then hers afterward — all for a roomful of mouldy grain!"

Deep into his firm throat-flesh drove the vise-grip of the half-breed's fingers, feeling out the carotid and the windpipe with the instinctive skill of an anatomist, and bringing awful pressure to bear upon them.

In dumb agony, his breath shut off, Guy struggled as vainly as might a wasp that is caught on flypaper. The all-powerful left arm held him fast-pinioned. The right hand's iron fingers were strangling him to death.

The room turned dirty red. It seemed to revolve. Manell's tongue protruded, feeling swollen to the size of a ham. His lungs were bursting. Fiery pains and splashes of rainbow light tore through his head.

Then, at once, his brain was clear. It seemed to have risen independently above his helpless and tortured body, and to function with wondrous clarity. Summoning his flagging muscles all to his aid, he jerked free his left upper-arm from where it was crushed less tightly than the other against the giant's breast.

By a miracle he freed it. In practically the same gesture, he brought down the lower edge of its stiffened open palm upon the nose-bridge of the swarthy face so close to his own. It was an old ruse, described to him, years agone, by his boxing-and-wrestling teacher, veteran of many a street-brawl.

Such a blow, delivered choppingly and with the open hand held taut, can do things to the bridge of an adversary's nose which are neither pleasant nor bearable. For one thing, the effect is half-blinding. For another, it is briefly numbing to brain and to motion.

Twice and thrice, in lightning succession and with all his tortured force, Manell smote thus downward upon the nose-bridge of his victor. He struck the three blows as quickly as a cook chops meat for hash.

Chapter 28

The half-breed shook him madly, and sought to tighten his own grip on body and throat. But, under that volley of open-handed chops, his grasp slackened involuntarily.

By supreme struggle, Manell tore free his swollen throat from the strangling fingers. His foot touching ground at the same moment, he drove his heel, with all its weight and momentum, down upon the instep of the giant.

Now, as every thug knows, the instep is one of the most important and acutely hurtable of all the body's various nerve-centers. A hard enough blow upon it will cause unconsciousness to the average man. This, too, Guy's old boxing preceptor had taught him. The half-forgotten knowledge stood him in grand stead.

Width a hoarse roar of agony, the half-breed relaxed for an instant his grasp. Guy reeled free from it, and sucked in a great breath of air to ease his tormented lungs.

That was all he had scope to do. Reckless with dizzy pain, maddened past all thought of caution, the giant was upon him again. His outflung arms were gathering Guy into their murder-embrace before Guy could avoid them.

But now Manell had scope to make use of his

wrestling lore, thanks to the other's insane fury. Deftly, as the great arms clamped him, he dived in. And he secured the hold he had sought.

His arms entwined the half-breed's thick body, his hands locking at the small of his enemy's back, at the base of the spine. The top of his head burrowed into the giant's throat, directly beneath the chin.

Manell had gained the underhold; perhaps the most dreaded grip in all rough-and-tumble warfare, if its user has the strength and the skill to make good his advantage. It is a simple problem in leverage — a problem as simple as it is insurmountable.

Modern professional wrestlers know, sometimes, tricks for breaking this terrible hold. The half-breed was a savage, not a modern professional.

Steadily, and with all his wiry strength, Guy drew his own locked hands toward him, as they pressed deep and deeper into the other's spine. Simultaneously, he drove the top of his head more and more persistently into the half-breed's neck and up against his under-chin; bracing his feet against the floor with the unshakable steadiness of the rock itself.

The half-breed fought madly to rip free from the trap. He sought to tear loose by superior strength. But that strength was cramped and stultified by his own back-thrust head and forward-drawn diaphragm.

He slugged with his hammer-fists at Manell's

tense body. But he could reach only the tight-muscled back and the rear of the head. Nor could he strike these with any telling force, because of their posture and of his own strained position. He swayed from one side to the other, stamping to crush the braced feet of the man who was exerting such awful double pressure on him. He strove to shift his back-strained throat so as to loose his chin from that pressure. But there was no room for such motion. His head was bent so far back that further turning was impossible.

Unrestingly and irresistibly, Manell was drawing the half-breed's spine toward him and was thrusting his neck backward. His own muscles ached and burned. He was panting hard for breath. But he set his teeth as he called upon himself for every remaining ounce of effort.

Then, the half-breed ceased to writhe and pitch and strike. With a snakelike motion he reached back to his hip.

Klyda screamed a shrill warning to Manell, as she saw a sheath-knife glint in the flashlight-radiance. She sprang forward to catch with her bare hands the descending knife-blade as the half-breed drove it slantingly downward at Manell's unprotected back.

Before she could reach him, the big hand opened convulsively. There was a muffled cracking sound. The knife tinkled harmlessly to the floor. The giant body slumped, inert and quivering like a shot rabbit, in Manell's clasp. Then, as Guy released his death-hold, the half-breed slid to the ground. His neck was broken.

Guy swayed drunkenly above him, fighting for breath and for strength to stand upright. The whole battle had occupied but a handful of seconds; yet it seemed to the exhausted man that he had been fighting in anguish and at constant peril to his life for hours. Scarcely could he feel Klyda's solicitous touch on his aching arm, or hear her pleading voice asking if he were harmed.

Then, from the floor came a diversion. Throughout Guy's brief fight with the half-breed, Gray Dawn and the Shoshone had been pitching deliriously about in a right unloving embrace, the dog still trying industriously to reach his foe's jugular, and rending at the hands and forearms wherewith the Indian sought to thrust him away.

Now, at the edge of the stair-well, the Shoshone succeeded in gripping the collie by the ruff, on either side of the slashing red jaws. Holding him thus, the Indian lurched to his feet. Lifting the seventy-pound dog bodily by this ruff-hold, he flung him back among the piles of bags.

With catlike speed Gray Dawn recovered his footing. He scrambled loose from the encumbering sacks, and whizzed back to the assault.

But the Shoshone had made good use of the moment's surcease. He had cast one panic glance at his dead comrade. Then, with a single breakneck leap he had disappeared down the stairway. The pad-pad-pad of his flying footfalls came back, curiously magnified by the echo, yet ever fainter as he bounded down the interminable flights, to safety.

The Indian had had quite enough of the adventure. There could be no fear of his returning to the scene of carnage, to face alone the raging collie and the man who, bare-handed, had slain his friend.

Guy stared down the dark stair-well. Then he went shakily across to where his fallen pistol lay. He picked it up and stood again by the stairhead, listening to the receding sound of bare feet running at full speed. Wearily, he faced the girl.

For an instant he peered at her, as she stood looking up at him in wide-eyed hero-worship. Blinking, he looked more closely at her.

Something was the matter with his eyes; something that made him see queerly. For Klyda seemed to be standing in a shimmering golden mist, which shone all about her like living sunshine. Around her dainty head flickered a halo of gold. Upon her hair and shoulders and clothes were drifts of glittering particles that gave back the flashlights' rays in a thousand showers of light. At her feet was a little heap of the same glimmering golden dust. She was surrounded by an aureate rain.

Frowning, he rubbed his eyes, so dispel the illusion. But, when he looked again, he saw the same phenomenon. From above, sifted down a shower of gleaming dust that irradiated her from head to foot.

Now she was brushing at flecks of the dust that had fallen on her flushed cheek and her eyelashes. Drawing away her hand and glancing at it, her face took on the same dumb look of bewilderment that marked Guy's.

Upward she looked, to locate the source of the shining dust-rain. Manell's eyes followed hers. Turned to stone, they gazed mutely.

The half-breed's bullet had rent a hole through one of the decayed planks which ceiled the vast room. Through this hole was trickling a steady little streamlet of pale golden dust. For some time the trickle had continued, if one might judge from the double handful heap of scintillant particles at Klyda's feet.

Manell broke from his unbelieving lethargy and bent down, scooping into his palm an ounce or so of the dust. Carrying it to the nearest flashlight, he bent over it. He felt it between his fingers and between his lips. He turned it this way and that, in the sharp flare of the electric torch. Then he babbled:

"Gold! *Flour*-gold! The — the purest and finest quality of gold. It's — it's raining — GOLD!"

"Don't you see?" cried the girl, her voice athrill with a sudden discovery. "This room was just the granary. The treasure chamber was between those planks and the stone roof above. It was hidden there, in case the mountain should be stormed. That bullet tore right into the gold-heap. It is pouring out on us! Guy, don't you see?"

Then, as her eye fell on the silent form huddled on the floor near the stair-head, the brightness faded from her face.

"Oh, Guy!" she murmured, hiding her face in his breast. "Here we've been exulting over — over what we have stumbled on, while — ! Oh, take me away, dear! I'm — I'm afraid!"

Chapter 29

It was a week later. Guy and Klyda were sitting on the veranda, at sunset. Gray Dawn as usual was lying at his master's feet. The man and his sweetheart had fallen silent. They were looking out at the grim mountain that glowed tenderly in the roseate light. Their hands were enlaced. The girl's head was on Guy's broad shoulder. Life was very wonderful. Their happiness seemed too full to be marred by mere words.

It was Gray Dawn that broke the sweet spell of dream-stillness.

The collie started up, suddenly, a deep growl in his furry throat, his silver hackles abristle. The curved tusks were glinting from beneath his back-curled lip. The Reverend Wilberforce, drowsing in a crotch of the orange tree, was wakened by the sound, and began to scold, grouchily, in his falsetto voice.

"Quiet, there, both of you!" ordered Manell, glowering annoyedly from the dog to the raccoon, vexed that their noise should intrude on the peace of the hour.

Then he saw that Dawn was staring fixedly at something. The next instant, the collie bounded off the porch, with a fanfare of barks. Calling him sharply back and bidding him lie down, Guy looked about, to learn the cause of the alarm. Advancing toward them from the gate was a man; tall, well-clad, light of step. Guy looked twice before he recognized the spruce figure as Tawakwina's.

The Shoshone continued to advance, until he came to the foot of the veranda steps. There was no embarrassment in his manner as he removed his hat and saluted the man and girl who were eyeing him so wonderingly.

"I am leaving California, tomorrow," began the Shoshone. "And I have called to pay my respects and my farewells to the winner of the duel."

"The duel?" echoed Guy.

"The duel with Grudge Mountain," answered Tawakwina. "Also it has occurred to me that you may one day be inquisitive as to some of the details of your victory. It is well to gratify curiosity. Especially when one has caused so much of it as have I and mine. And when that day comes, I may not be at hand to answer your questions."

"I don't understand."

"You see, I am leaving not only California but America as well. America is no place for us aboriginal Americans. In France I shall probably be received in fairly good society. As Cubans and South Americans and negroes are. I may even acquire the title of *le beau sauvage* or something equally flattering. I have money enough to live there or anywhere else, in considerable comfort, you know."

"You — ?"

"The hoard contained enough for us both. I have taken my share. I have given enough to my brother to make him a well-to-do rancher, in Mexico. My brother, by the way, was the Indian who had some slight difference with your dog, the night you killed this young lady's uncle."

He spoke with complete unconcern. But at his last words, Klyda exclaimed:

"My uncle? What do you mean? I —"

"You didn't know?" asked Tawakwina, a hint of surprise in his deep voice. "Why, from your being out here with your father, I gather that your grandfather broke his oath and told. In so telling, he made no mention of — ? But then, of course, he couldn't. His child was not born until seven months after he was sent away. There was no way he could know. But surely you must have noticed the strange likeness between your father and his half-brother, Isharoyi! He —"

"I don't understand any of this!" declared Guy, perplexed. "Do you mean to say — ?"

"As I told you," returned Tawakwina, courteously, "that is why I came here today. I owe you my life. I tried to pay a portion of the debt by persuading Isharoyi to wait, before killing you. When I could not make him wait out the week, I brought you a message to go in two days. I persuaded him to give you that much chance. When we saw the sheet tied to the orange tree, we all three thought you had surrendered. That is why we relaxed our guard. Only when the signal cord was pulled, as you climbed the stairs

257

to the treasure-loft, did Isharoyi and my brother Hani, know. Then they ran from our house to destroy you. I was from home that night. Thus I was saved the black choice of fighting against my own uncle and my brother or against the man who had saved me from death. I am grateful."

"Your uncle and your brother?" interposed Guy. "Say, would you mind telling me this thing, from the beginning?"

"As I told you, that is why I am here, today. From the oath-breaking revelations of this young lady's unsainted grandfather, you know already the old story of the treasure and its keepers. In this latter day, the keepers had shrunk from thousands of priests to one. That one was Isharoyi. He was half-white. And yet in him alone burned the ancient zeal. So when my grandfather died, he bequeathed to him the office of high-priest. Hani and I are the sons of my grandfather's only son. Neither of us could learn to feel the sacredness of the old faith. To us it seemed petty and outworn."

"It is. Go ahead."

"In the hope of making me worthy to follow in his footsteps, Isharoyi sent me to Carlisle and then to Oxford, to educate me. But the more I was educated the less I wished to succeed to the dead-and-gone priesthood of an extinct faith. It was so, also, with Hani, though he adored my uncle. Hani is a stupid blanket-Indian. Not like me. Hani and I took the oath, in babyhood — my people's immemorial oath — to serve the high-priest, to the death. But the high-priest is dead. You killed him."

"In fair fight."

"In fair fight," assented Tawakwina. "I grant that. Hani told me. At Isharoyi's command, I wrote those silly warnings. I pinned one of them to your chest while you slept. At his command, I took service with you. Because of my oath. That is why I gave Jenner $100 to leave the job open to me by pretending he was scared away. (It was easy to pick an acquaintance with him — and it was easier to bribe him.) That is why I helped Isharoyi and Hani, all one night, to destroy your new vineyard. That is why Hani stole the golden bullet from your doorstep. That is why he set fire to Mr. Graeme's home and killed his live-stock.

"But now Isharoyi is dead. With him die the priesthood and the old creeds and the obsolete oaths. Hani and I are free. And we rejoice that our lives are no longer bound on the altar of a dead priesthood."

"I don't blame you. This is the twentieth century."

"By the way, Miss Graeme," resumed Tawakwina, ignoring Guy's interruption, "I owe you an apology for frightening you. We saw you and your father come to the mountain, one morning, and then separate to find the more quickly the groove to the ledge; — the groove which Isharoyi later filled with rocks, by means of the Inca-levers. Isharoyi said he would kill your father with stones, as he climbed. He bade me frighten you away, lest you witness the killing, and tell how it was done. I threw a meal sack over my head and shoulders and crawled toward you, through the rocks, on all fours. Then, as you pointed your bijou little pistol at me, I heard this collie bark. And I knew he would attack me if he saw me. Most collies hate Indians. So I hid."

"It was you who — ?"

"Yes. I am sorry. The time is past for me to play so foolish a role, or indeed any role. I am free. Unless," he hesitated, "unless Mr. Manell should seek to hold me to the Shoshone oath of allegiance I swore to him, in my first delirium of reaction, when he drew me back from death on the ledge."

"No, thanks," laughed Guy. "I've no use for a slave. I absolve you. Besides, we are going east as soon as Mr. Graeme can travel."

"I suppose so," said Tawakwina. "Well, then I am not the only person the treasure is to make happy, nor is Hani. It has waited through the centuries, doing no good to anyone and causing many deaths. Until Isharoyi drew from it to educate me, it lay as it had lain since the Incas hoarded it."

"It was really the Incas, then?"

"So the tale goes. You know, they did not hoard it as treasure alone, but as material for their temple implements and images and as utensils for their priests, and as weapons. (Yes, as weapons. Though the tempering of gold to steel-strength is long since a lost art, like making glass malleable.) That is why there was but a trifle more than three hundred thousand dollars' worth of it left in the little cache above the granary. The cache you discovered by means of the bullet hole and that you have been rifling all week, since then. There was a little more than two hundred thousand dollars' worth of dust in the crypt under the onyx god, in the temple. I have taken that, for Hani and myself. It is enough for us. You are welcome to what you found. The hoard can be put to better use by all three of us, than for the molding of sacred gold bullets — bullets which are supposed to bear a charm against invaders of the mountain, but which miss one victim and only break the leg of another."

"Isharoyi fired both of them?"

"Yes. But the old creed had lost its power — that or else Isharoyi's aim was bad. Yet he was always threatening to kill. He even threatened to kill me when I stood between you and him, that morning when his flung stone had knocked you senseless."

"It *was* Isharoyi, then! The stone-thrower? I thought —"

"I had to tell him the stone had crushed your skull and that we were taking you home to die, Hani and myself. He would have killed you, even then, if I had not made him believe you could not live an hour. At last he let us bear your 'dead' body to your doorstep and leave it there to frighten the Graemes away. It was a terrible scene, in that lower chamber, with you lying unconscious and he struggling to get at your throat with his gold knife. There was a more terrible scene, later, when he found we had deceived him, and that you lived. It was then that he refused to wait out the week; and I threw the note to you. I am glad there can be no more such scenes."

He held out his hand, almost timidly, to Guy, who grasped it.

"Mr. Manell," said the Shoshone. "You are a good deal of a man. And it is you who have freed me from bondage. Good-by. May life hold much happiness for you."

Abruptly he turned away. Without glancing back, he strode across the meadow and out of sight. Mutely, the lovers looked after his receding dark figure.

Gray Dawn got up and stretched, fore and aft. Then he yawned aloud, his pink mouth a white-fringed cavern. But the two humans were too engrossed with each other to take the broad hint. There were none but themselves, in this world of theirs.

c